Counting CANDLES

DUSTIN W. BRADSHAW

SWEETWATER
BOOKS
An Imprint of Cedar Fort, Inc.
Springville, Utah

ISBN 13: 978-1-4621-1433-7

Published by Sweetwater Books, an imprint of Cedar Fort, Inc.
2373 W. 700 S., Springville, UT 84663
Distributed by Cedar Fort, Inc., www.cedarfort.com

LIBRARY OF CONGRESS CATALOGING-IN-PUBLICATION DATA

Bradshaw, Dustin, author.
Counting candles / Dustin W. Bradshaw.
pages cm
Summary: James Smith is anxious about his life and his family on his fortieth birthday, but experiences a change in attitude.
ISBN 978-1-4621-1433-7 (pbk.)
1. Birthdays--Fiction. 2. Anxiety--Fiction. 3. Worry--Fiction. I. Title.

PS3602.R342853C68 2014
813'.6--dc23

2013050926

Cover design by Kristen Reeves
Cover design © 2014 by Lyle Mortimer
Edited and typeset by Melissa J. Caldwell

Printed in the United States of America

10 9 8 7 6 5 4 3 2 1

Counting CANDLES

Praise for ***Counting Candles***

"*Counting Candles* raises our hope that ordinary folk like you and I can do extraordinary things!"

FARINA MCCARTHY-STONEX, Marriage and Family Counselor, Brigham Young University-Hawaii

"*Counting Candles* will be the best book you read this year. . . . Dustin Bradshaw, a gifted storyteller, perceives the cracks in our economy and leads his characters right to their edges. Too often we have seen those we know and love fall between the cracks. And this is the underlying tension in *Counting Candles*. We know what to expect—failure—and we keep reading hoping for a better ending. His good characters, as with the good people we know, sometimes jump the divide. I have no doubt that once you start *Counting Candles*, you will read it to the end."

JOHN GUBBINS, author of *Profound River* and *Raven's Fire*

"Dustin Bradshaw's *Counting Candles* provides a gentle, yet poignant reminder of the amazing power to be found in doing good."

RYAN RAPIER, author of *The Reluctant Blogger*

"Bradshaw's *Counting Candles* is very much reminiscent of *It's a Wonderful Life*, where a man who believes his life is ordinary and unsuccessful discovers that the complete opposite is true. In his novel, Bradshaw develops a host of characters so effectively that by the end of the book, readers believe that they, in fact, know each one of these people personally. The book captures a timeless element of human desire—the need to feel that your time here on earth is worthwhile—and because of that, *Counting Candles* will be just as pertinent ten or twenty years from now as it is today. *Counting Candles* is a delightful and recommended read."

AMIE JANE LEAVITT, author of *A Daredevil's Guide to Swimming with Sharks*

For my Lady and my Lucky Dragon

1

James Smith

The most extraordinary experiences of life happen to the most ordinary people in the most ordinary moments. James Smith certainly did not feel like an extraordinary person at this particular moment. Right then, his head was buried under his pillow in a futile attempt to escape a spiteful alarm clock.

"Already?" James grudgingly reached over to silence the blaring siren. The clock's lime-green numbers illuminated the otherwise dark room in an eerie haze, indicating a time of 5:30 in the morning. He rolled over, groggy from too few hours of sleep.

It was moments like these that the softness of the mattress and the warmth of the comforter tempted James to stay in bed. Whatever happened to being a teenager and having the option to sleep in, at least on Saturdays? In his youth he assumed he would grow out of wanting to sleep in when he became an adult, but now he knew the truth: the "grown-ups" only get up early out of a sense of duty and then pretend they enjoy it to instill the same sense of duty in their children. James rubbed his eyes and sighed. Peeling back the comforter in one sweep, he allowed the chill of the spring air to shock his system. Molly, his wife of thirteen years, groaned in sleepy discomfort as she rolled away, curling the blankets closer to remedy the sudden exposure. James always got out of bed first. He knew Molly hated mornings even more than he did. Waking up frequently during the night with their three children over the years had only increased her desire to stay in bed.

In his head, James counted, *One, two, three!*—something he often did to prepare his mind and body to do something they both were revolting against. Unpleasant tasks always seemed easier if done all at once. *Duty*, James thought. *I am doing this out of a sense of duty.* On the count of three, he stood up and staggered to the bathroom, using the green light of the clock as a guide.

He waited until after the door was closed to turn on the bright lights. This was a habit he'd learned the hard way. About a week into their marriage, he had turned on the light in the early morning to find a lost shoe he needed for work. His new bride, who was normally even-tempered and quiet, had turned into an angry bear disturbed out of hibernation. He had been careful ever since to not make that mistake again.

The light blinded his weary eyes. He steadied himself by placing one hand lightly on the sink and pinching his eyes shut until they adjusted.

Once James opened his eyes, he found himself looking straight into the mirror. His light brown hair was a bit long—he needed a haircut. The speckles of gray in his hair and beard, along with the dark rings around his eyes, reminded him that he was aging. Molly, a trained nurse practitioner, had told him in her cheerful, informative voice that "aging is part of life. Your cells are not reproducing and repairing as fast as they were when you were younger. The sagging, aching, failing organs are just products of the phenomenon." James snorted a laugh now as he looked at himself, just as he had done when she had told him. Was that supposed to make him feel better? Because it didn't.

But James knew that Molly was the most sincere and kind person he had ever known. She wasn't trying to make him uncomfortable; she just loved her career. It was in her nature to spout information like that. He had become accustomed to it, though it frequently felt like he was walking around with a medical textbook. After his earlier comment to Molly about how he was aging, he had learned how some people look younger than they are because their skin has more collagen. Molly also added that those same people don't heal the same, and as a result, keloids, caused by more collagen, create more scarring and scar tissue after an accident. "Nobody is perfect, James," she had said, kissing him on the cheek as she went off.

"No, nobody is perfect," James said out loud to the mirror while absentmindedly touching his cheek where Molly had kissed him. "Definitely not me."

James looked up at the words along the top of the mirror. Molly had joined the word craze and had her favorite inspirational sayings printed in fancy lettering strategically placed around the house. This one read, "YOU MAKE A DIFFERENCE." He didn't know why she had chosen that phrase for them both to read every morning when they dressed for work, but right now it caused a hollow pit in his stomach.

The words reminded him of the very worries he had been feeling all week: Do I do enough? Have I done enough? This weekend he was turning forty years old. James sighed.

He had nothing against getting older, theoretically. But with the celebrated "big day" coming up, he had begun to reevaluate his life. He realized, returning his gaze to his average, graying reflection in the mirror, that he could sum his forty years of life up into two depressing twin words: *mundane* and *mediocre*.

He was turning forty years old, and what did he have to show for it? Nothing.

James once again read the words on the mirror and wondered if he did make a difference. Nothing worth highlighting stuck out. Life was just life.

He heard the floor creak in the bedroom, signifying that Molly was on her way to wake the kids. He hurried into the shower. He had wasted enough time already.

2

James Smith

"*James, will you* finish getting Noah ready? I need to finish my hair," Molly asked as he walked downstairs.

"Sure can!" James called back. He scanned for Noah, their three-year-old. Noah was really growing fast, his little playful personality surfacing. "Where's my little man?" James called as he walked into the living room. He heard a laugh from the other side of the couch. As he approached, an excited squeal came from Noah, and he turned to run into the dining room away from James.

"Where do you think you're going?" James laughed as he sped up to catch the toddler. Noah looked back and howled with laughter as he ran faster. In three big leaps, James caught Noah, both of them laughing.

"I fas'! Daddy, I fas'!" Noah exclaimed as he wrapped his short arms around James's neck.

"You are fast. I almost didn't catch you!"

Noah's face turned serious, and he looked James in the

eye. James watched the little face, inches away from his own, process something serious. Finally, Noah reached up and put a sticky hand on either side of James's face. "Daddy, you fas' too. We bof fas'!" James smiled at his son's kindness.

"Thank you, little guy. I'm glad we can both be fast. Now let's get you ready for the day." He put Noah down and dressed him in the blue shirt Molly had laid out.

"Tank 'oo!"

"You're welcome, my little man!" James smiled and tousled Noah's thick hair before he pulled away. James stayed crouched on his knees for a few minutes as Noah bounced away, singing some of his own words to the tune of his favorite television show. There was so much joy in his little body. It was like that for all their kids. He wondered where all the joy went in adulthood. James hoped that he and Molly could keep their three children happy as long as possible.

If there was one thing James was proud of in his life, it was his children. All three of them had turned out to be outstanding and polite—although he knew Molly had more to do with that than he did.

Molly had chosen to quit work and stay home after she gave birth to their oldest son, Jaden, more than ten years ago. She unexpectedly found a new joy and satisfaction in educating their children herself. Three years later, their princess, Natalee, had been born. Molly had stayed home with the children until this last year, when she'd had to return to work.

Again, guilt seeped in and choked out the joy James had felt moments earlier, filling him with apprehension. It was his fault that little Noah wouldn't have the same experience Jaden and Natalee had had with their mother being home and available all the time. As the head accountant for a midsize import and export company called Near World, he had been brought into a conversation with the board of directors several months ago. The conversation had been solemn and brief: Near World was struggling with the slow economy, and Mr. Barnes, the company president, had said it was time to make some cuts. They had done all they could businesswise to avoid this course of action, but the numbers weren't rising as they wanted them to. They were preparing to lay off over one hundred personnel within the week.

Alarmed, James had spoken up during the meeting and offered a different solution. His proposed plan was to ask all of the high-level salaried employees if they would be willing to take a ten percent pay cut this year in order to avoid firing anyone. The board had liked the option and had given the employees that would be affected the opportunity to vote. Of course, nobody was going to be selfish enough to disagree, and the program was put into place immediately after the vote. James was lauded as a hero in the company, which was a credit to Mr. Barnes's humble leadership style since he could've easily taken the credit. However, somehow James did not feel like a hero.

He remembered coming home that night after the vote. The idea had been a spur-of-the-moment response during the meeting, but he was now realizing that he should have kept his mouth shut. Yes, it saved jobs for several families, but the reality was that the ten percent pay cut would stretch his own family's budget even further—and it was already fraying at the seams.

As he explained to Molly what had happened, she knew the blow their finances had taken without him telling her. She offered to start working again without hesitation. James knew she wanted to stay home with Noah just as much as she did with the other children, but he had no other alternative. They both knew she needed to go back to work. James had felt defeated that day and every day since when Molly left for work in her medical clothing. Molly insisted she wanted to go back to work, and James tried to tell himself that, but somewhere in the back of his mind he felt like he was failing to provide for his family.

"James?" Molly called down the stairs as if she could hear his thoughts. "Can you drop the kids off at school on your way to work? I'll take Noah to Jessica's. I have the early shift today and won't have time to do both."

"Of course," James called back. Molly's longtime friend Jessica happened to live nearby and was more than willing to babysit Noah for a small fee while Molly was at work. The heavy feeling in James's heart increased as he thought about Molly having to leave Noah with Jessica. It wasn't that James was opposed to Molly working; he just wanted it to be her choice to work, not a necessity because he couldn't handle it.

James finally stood up and walked into the kitchen to help Jaden and Natalee collect all their books as they got ready for school. He looked around the modest kitchen. It was not that Molly and James had put themselves into unnecessary debt—in fact, they had tried hard *not* to be careless with money. Their home was a three-bedroom Cape with an average-sized yard located in the all-too-familiar cookie-cutter suburbia that surrounded nearly every city in the United States.

Molly deserves more than this, he thought. His marriage was the most important part of his life, and he wished he could do more to show Molly that. If he had been more successful in his career, she would have had more and wouldn't have had to worry about working. If she wanted to work, it would be for her to achieve her own goals, not to make up where he lacked.

"Natalee, Jaden! Let's go! You're going to be late!" James called to the two older children, who were running around collecting missing pieces of clothing and school supplies.

He saw Jaden's book bag sitting on one of the dining room chairs, and he moved over to put in the books he had collected. As he fit them all in, he saw that the science book had a large picture of Albert Einstein on the back. The picture brought a sudden memory to his mind. During his undergraduate studies, James had written an essay on the fact that Einstein was a celebrated scientist throughout the world. He had argued that, while Einstein's contributions to science were invaluable, where he had succeeded in science he had failed with his family. Now reminded of Einstein's life in shocking juxtaposition to his own, James thought that at least Einstein had succeeded in one or the other. James, on the other hand, was failing in both.

James had finally rounded up Jaden and all his belongings, and they were both standing at the front door waiting for Natalee. "Natalee! What are you doing? We're going to be late!"

Her small, girlish whine came from her bedroom upstairs. "I can't find my pink shoes!" James normally thought that Natalee's obsessions with fashion and the color pink were funny and cute, but the humor waned when they were running late.

"There's a pair of shoes right here." He gestured to the black shoes sitting by the front door as if she could see him pointing to them.

"Dad!" she called back, full of exasperation. "Those are black!" James looked down and wondered how she knew which shoes he was referring to.

"What's wrong with black, Princess?" James called up the stairs, trying unsuccessfully to keep the mirth out of his voice.

"Dad!" the disparaged voice called down. "Black is so old-fashioned!"

James gasped in mock horror. "I wear black shoes every

day! Are you saying I'm old fashioned? Should I get some pink shoes?"

"That's not funny!"

James had to laugh despite himself. He turned to Jaden. "She's only seven! What's it going to be like when she's seventeen?" Jaden smirked and shook his head as if in disbelief. James noted how handsome his oldest son was becoming.

Molly rounded the top of the stairs and hurried down toward them. "Nat, honey, black shoes will be fine. You're going to be late."

"Okay," came the defeated reply, and Natalee followed her mother down the stairs.

James watched his beautiful wife walk down the stairs. It made him so happy that she had taken a chance on him and married him. As she neared the bottom of the stairs where James and Jaden stood, James teased, "I wish it was that easy for me. Must be your good looks."

Molly let out an impromptu laugh as she dashed across the living room to scoop up Noah and meet them back at the door. "Thanks for taking them, James. I love you. See you tonight at practice." She leaned in and gave him a kiss, to which both Jaden and Natalee, apparently forgetting about her shoes, squealed in mock disgust.

"What? You don't like that your parents love each other?" Molly jokingly chided them, and just to make her point, she leaned in for another kiss. Both James and Molly broke into laughter as their children howled in protest again.

Noah even joined in and pushed James's face away. "Mumma, love me!" A wave of affection passed through James as he backed up to let his family out the door.

"Yes, your mom loves you too, little guy." He gave him a kiss on his forehead. "See you both tonight."

After finally getting Jaden and Natalee in the car, James looked at the clock on the dashboard. It was 7:45. Just enough time to get to the school and then to work. He traced the exact routes in his mind as he backed out of his little plot of suburbia. Suddenly Natalee broke his train of thought.

"Dad! You forgot Mr. Scheimer's paper!"

James groaned to himself. He didn't have time for Mr. Scheimer's paper.

Mr. Gerald Scheimer had been their next-door neighbor for the ten years that James and Molly had lived here. Mr. Scheimer had been old when they had moved in, so by now he was ancient. His family had moved out of state, and he lived in his large home—one much larger than their own—all by himself. Molly and James had tried to befriend him by inviting him to family parties and summer barbecues in the backyard. He would often come, but he was a little standoffish and cold with the kids. His gruff complaints were the worst when the kids played on his lawn.

For all these years, James had retrieved the daily paper from the end of the driveway—where the lazy delivery boy carelessly threw it—and walked it to Mr. Scheimer's door. Mr. Scheimer always watched from his glass storm door for James to arrive. He never thanked James or said a kind word. He usually greeted James with, "You're late today. Bad night's sleep?" or "Your lawn needs clipping. It's an eyesore."

Day after day, it was the same routine. James waited for the moment when it was different—that golden moment when Mr. Scheimer would actually say something nice or friendly. James was not sure anymore of when he had started delivering Mr. Scheimer's paper to the door for him or even why he started doing it, for that matter. But now it was part of his morning routine. In the rush of the morning, he had forgotten to do it today. James was tempted to just make a lame excuse and be on his way. But he looked in the rearview mirror at Natalee's brow, furrowed in genuine concern. Jaden was already spotting the paper on the sidewalk.

He thought of Einstein again. James knew they would be late, but he was not going to let his kids down. Duty won for the second time that morning. With a twinge of determination, James stopped the car and jumped out. Once he knew he was out of earshot, he grumbled, "He doesn't even appreciate it." But even as he said it, James knew he did this as much for his children's sake as Mr. Scheimer's.

He scooped up the paper and made three large leaping steps to the door. Mr. Scheimer wasn't there. *Odd*, James thought. Mr. Scheimer rarely missed a day waiting for his paper. Actually, now that James thought about it, he couldn't recall ever having a morning when Mr. Scheimer wasn't already at the door. Then, looking on the bright side of the situation, he figured that at least he didn't have to hear a snide comment this morning. He was having enough depressing thoughts today without someone else piling them on. He went back to the car in a light jog, and when he saw the faces of his two children watching him expectantly, he was relieved that he had made the right choice.

3

James Smith

After dropping off the children, James meandered his way through the city to the Near World offices in the business district downtown. "Another day . . . another ordinary day," he mumbled to himself as he drove out of the light rain into the underground parking garage. He grabbed his umbrella and headed out into the busy city street. Every day as he made this walk, particularly in the rain, James questioned why Near World had never invested in an entrance from the garage to the building. He speculated various reasons: having only one entrance made the building more secure, or Near World's board of directors wanted its employees to get at least five minutes of exercise a day.

Normally, James enjoyed the walk from the garage to the office doors. The old 1920s architecture was ornate and beautiful, and he enjoyed the peacefulness of the morning air. Today, however, the weather was dreary, matching

James's mood. He skirted puddles in the uneven pavement and changed his usual lazy stroll into a sprint.

He ducked under cover at the well-lit glass doors, which boasted the ornate, embossed logo of Near World. As he shook his umbrella, the doors opened to reveal a portly doorman—his smile a rare bright spot in the gloomy day.

"Good morning, Mr. James," the rich voice greeted him.

James looked up and couldn't help his own smile surfacing. "Hello, Hal. How are you?" For as long as James could remember, Hal had been the doorman for the Near World building. Just like today, he always wore a smile. James had made friends with Hal months ago during a rainstorm. James had forgotten an umbrella and had stood in the large building entry for an hour waiting for the rain to calm enough for him to make it to the parking garage without getting soaked. Hal had stood right next to him, like a stalwart captain not willing to abandon his crew during a storm.

They had told stories about growing up and laughed until their guts ached. Since that day, James had relished the three-minute conversations he had with Hal each day as James went in and out of the Near World doors.

"I'm splendid, Mr. James. Doesn't the rain smell wonderful?" Hal used to call James "Mr. Smith," but after months of persuasion, Hal had finally reverted to "Mr. James." "You deserve some respecting," Hal had told him one day in a this-conversation-is-over tone of voice. James figured "Mr. James" could work. It was at least a slight improvement over the formality of his last name.

"I suppose it does," James said, smiling again. Hal had the talent of finding the good in everything, even a dreary day. "Have a good day, Hal. You're a good man. See you at lunchtime?"

"I'll be right here, Mr. James. Don't you worry—I'll be right here." Hal's teasing tone made James chuckle.

James made his way up to the seventh floor, where his office was located. He scanned the cubicles as he passed, making a mental note of which employees in the accounting department had made it to work on time.

James made a point to say hello to each of them by name as he passed their cubicles. It wasn't much, but he wanted to let them know he acknowledged them and appreciated the work they did. He slowed as he arrived at the desk of their new intern, Enric. "Enric, how're you doing?"

Enric must have been concentrating on what he was working on because he startled, nearly hitting his head on the cabinet above his computer. "Ah . . . I'm . . . uh, I'm fine."

James smiled. "I didn't mean to scare you. I was just checking in to see if you needed anything."

"Yes, Mr. Smith. Thank you, I'm doing really well." Enric shifted slightly and straightened his tie with an unsteady hand.

James smiled again. Enric was obviously nervous. James wanted to reassure him. "I hear you're doing wonderful. Keep up the great work." He reached over and patted Enric on the shoulder and started toward his office again. "Oh, and Enric, I don't bite—at least not too hard—so no need to be so nervous when I stop by to say hello." Enric wasn't sure how to react at first, but when the other office staff started to giggle, he smiled and relaxed.

James's office had a row of windows overlooking his team. Next to the dark faux mahogany office door was a gold plaque that read:

James Smith, CPA
Chief Accountant
Near World

James hesitated as he entered. Long ago he had been told by Mrs. Jarat, an elderly friend, who lived down the street from his parents, that when you name children you should choose names that you want them to become. He could still hear her frail voice bragging, "That's why I named my son Rich, and he's a doctor now, richest person in the whole family." Her voice always raised in pitch, sound, and excitement when she said that. *Every time* she said it. She always added, "And my daughter is Elizabeth, you know, after the Queen of England." James thought about the fact that Elizabeth hadn't turned out to be the queen; she became a teacher. But that fact didn't seem to register with Mrs. Jarat, who never mentioned it in conversation.

James walked in and placed his wet umbrella and briefcase near the desk. He wondered what his parents had been thinking when they'd named him. Obviously they had not heard Mrs. Jarat's theories at that point. They named him James Smith. How much more bland could you get? Maybe Mrs. Jarat was right—he *had* become bland and mediocre. He didn't have too much to live up to with a name like James Smith.

He didn't even have a way to spice up his name. The nickname options were Jim, Jimmy, or Jamie. He had tried to be called all of those during his life, but for one reason or another none of them had stuck. Once he had searched the Internet for the most common names in the United States, and both James and Smith were not only *on* the list, but they were also number one. He was officially the most generic person out there. He was officially Mr. Average! James laughed quietly as he pictured a stone bust of himself pronouncing his self-awarded title. He could almost hear the announcers cry, "And now we have Mr. Average!" followed by the chorus of trumpets—dah, dun, dah, dah, DAH! James shook his head and turned to his work.

Throughout the morning, James kept busy, trying to drown out his thoughts by working on a project that was due later in the day. When his phone buzzed sometime around midday, he ignored it. It buzzed again. James glanced over in irritation to see who it was. The large phone, much more technical than he thought was necessary, brightly displayed the caller's name: Betty.

Betty was his determined administrative assistant. She had worked with Near World longer than anyone he knew. She must be nearing her sixtieth birthday—though nobody ever asked to confirm this—but she was just as spunky as she had ever been. She had been offered promotions several times over the years but had denied them all to stay where she was. She said she liked it. James was happy she didn't leave. She deserved to be promoted, but without her he was sure his office would fall to shambles. She was the sun the entire office revolved around. Most times James just told her what he needed and stayed out of the way. Betty ran the ship.

He pushed the speaker button. "Yes, Betty. What can I do for you?" Listening to himself, he wondered if the roles of boss and employee were blurred a bit when it came to his relationship with Betty.

"James, did you forget your lunch appointment?" Her scolding tone reminded him eerily of his mother as he glanced from the computer to the calendar on his phone. Sure enough, there it was: Lunch with Troy Walker, 1200 hours at City Diner. He had forgotten. He glanced at the clock on the computer: 11:45.

"Thanks, Betty. What would I ever do without you?"

"You'd have a messy desk and angry friends."

"I guess you're right," James said, smiling. Betty sure kept life in the office interesting. "That means you can't retire until I do."

"Honey, don't be saying that R word to me! And stop

your blabberin'. You're going to be late." The line went dead. James shook his head. If anyone else had hung up on him after a potentially offensive statement, he may have been insulted. But that was just Betty: quick, sharp, and to the point. He saved the file he was working on, grabbed his wallet with a sigh, and headed to City Diner a few blocks away. He had forgotten his umbrella, so he was lucky the rain had stopped when he stepped outside.

City Diner was James's favorite place to eat lunch. Everyone referred to it affectionately as "the Diner." It wasn't full of stuffy business professionals that thought too highly of themselves like the other restaurants downtown. The Diner had a more relaxed atmosphere, in large part due to the stereotypical 1940s diner culture it sustained.

James was actually the one that had suggested he and Troy eat there. Troy was James's first college roommate. He remembered going off to college as a fresh high school graduate, nervous about living with a stranger. Horrible roommate stories from college students he knew had put him on edge. He was thankful when he met a small-town boy full of life named Troy Walker. They had become fast friends their freshman year and chose to room together for their remaining years of college. The two of them had some fun memories.

James reached a street corner and saw that the blinking countdown sign for the pedestrians was counting down. Normally he would start walking faster to make it across the road before the light changed, but today he stopped and watched it finish: 5 . . . 4 . . . 3 . . . 2 . . . 1. Then the red hand signifying "stop" flashed.

He was not in a hurry to get to the Diner.

He knew Troy would be there prepared to eat already. Troy could always out-eat anyone in the dorm; being late for lunch was not an option for Troy—ever. James thought the worst part about Troy's overactive metabolism was that he never gained a pound of fat. Even now, years later, he looked like he was in his twenties.

Troy had called a few weeks ago to schedule a lunch. James winced when he remembered the conversation. "I wanted to call to get on your schedule early. I know you're busy, and I want to see you," Troy said. James had opened his calendar and found it painfully blank.

Putting on his happiest tone, he'd confirmed the appointment. He had since completely forgotten about it. He wasn't in the mood to try to be upbeat and happy today.

James debated about going back to the office to have Betty call and cancel. He could make up some kind of excuse about not being able to make it. But the scorn he would get from Betty was bound to be intense. He weighed his options, but by the time the light flashed the white pedestrian symbol, he knew an hour with Troy would be much less painful than hearing Betty chide him for the next several years about the time he had lied to his friend.

James really did like Troy. It wasn't often that Troy was in the city and had time for lunch. James knew it was petty that he did not want to go—it truly was. The real reason James was dragging he feet was that Troy was a successful businessman. He had, with his charming, energetic personality, worked his way up through the ranks and was the regional director of a big tech company. Troy's success—as represented by a big house, sleek car, and European vacations—seemed to highlight James's lack of all of the above.

James didn't consider himself materialistic. He never fretted about nice cars or clothing brands. Yet he did want to show that he could provide for his family. James's father provided a comfortable home for their family of seven. Why was it that James couldn't do that for his family of five, even when he tried to?

To put it simply, Troy had everything, and he made obtaining it all look so easy. He was like that all the way through college: while James had studied all night and into the weekend for average grades, Troy had aced tests without even trying—most of the time without even attending class. James stopped a few yards before the Diner's entrance and took a deep breath. Troy was one of his best, and most loyal, friends. Never once had Troy flaunted his success or treated James as a failure, so why was James acting as if it were Troy's fault? James knew it was his own issues. Troy deserved to receive friendship back.

James looked at the familiar Diner. The old building, with its cliché neon colors and chrome accents, was almost an eyesore against all of the beautiful stone architecture surrounding it. James took a deep breath and pushed the door open. The smell of grease and maple syrup assaulted his nose.

"James, old boy!" he heard Troy call over the din.

James turned to see Troy, dapper as ever in his perfectly tailored suit, waving frantically. He waved back and started over. Troy met him halfway with a huge bear hug, not at all worried about the awkward stares from the rest of the Diner customers. Troy landed three strong raps on James's back, laughing the whole time. "How're you doing, old boy?"

James, relieved to be out of the embrace, stepped back to catch his breath.

"I'm all right. You look good as ever," he said. James sincerely meant it. Troy looked amazing.

"Eh, it's just the suit. They cut it to make me look better than I am." Troy cast off the compliment and started back to the table with his right arm still around James's back. As they walked, James noted the mention of a custom-tailored suit.

"Thank you for taking time to have lunch with me," Troy said once they had settled into the overstuffed vinyl booth.

"Of course. I had nothing better to do." A small lie.

Troy laughed. "I know that's not true! How's life? How are Molly and the kids doing? I feel so bad that Sarah and I haven't been up to see you in months!"

James was thankful that Troy was staying on neutral ground—family. It was something they shared and nothing to compare. The playing field was equal in this category. "Molly is great as ever. She says she enjoys going back to work."

Even as he said it, James couldn't believe his own words. *Of all things to mention, that is what comes out first?* he chided himself. He hurried on before Troy could ask about it. "Jaden and Natalee are busy with school, and now baseball season has started. That's all we seem to do."

Troy cut in, "How is that team of yours doing anyway?"

"They're all right. We win some and lose some." Not entirely true either. So far his team had lost far more games than they had won.

"It's really great that you're doing that, James. I wish I had the talent you have to coach."

"I don't really think it's talent. It's more like there was nobody else to do it. I'm the coach by default. But the little guys sure are gritty; I have to give them that."

"Whatever, James. I guarantee you no other coach on that field watches coaching videos during the off-season on how to coach better."

But they win, James thought. Instead he said, "I do it for Jaden."

"Well, that's a good reason, if you ask me! Now, what's good in this joint? I'm starving." Troy opened the laminated menu that was just as tacky and cliché as the Diner's exterior.

The waitress came to the table. James looked up and saw that she was pretty. Her hair was pulled back into a bun, and her yellow diner uniform contrasted with her almond skin. Her name tag read *Shamanda*.

"Are you two ready to order? Or do you need a minute?"

"I'm ready. You ready?" Troy mumbled without looking up from his menu.

"All right. What can I get for you? My name is Shamanda, and I will be helping you today," the waitress said while tucking the empty drink tray under her arm and pulling out a small white pad of paper and a pen. Her tone sounded rote and hollow, making James look up again. This time, he saw that Shamanda's eyes looked heavy with sadness.

Troy shut his menu and looked up with his trademark smile. "Hello, Shamanda. How are you today?" James saw a flash of emotion cross Shamanda's face, and she blinked twice rapidly. Then it was gone. The hollow mask was back.

"I'm all right. Thank you for asking," she replied. To her credit, she even forced a faux smile onto her face. But the light in her eyes was completely out; they were a pool of hurt and distraction.

"Well, in that case, I'll have the daily special." Troy made his choice and shut his menu dramatically.

James chimed in, "Make that two. Thank you, Shamanda." His sympathy for the waitress, whom he didn't even know, was strong. Maybe it was because her eyes reflected the same burden of sadness and grief that he was lugging around today.

Shamanda left them, and the conversation turned to catching up on life—work, family, the weather, and updates on mutual friends.

James tried to make sure he was as kind as possible to Shamanda whenever she came to refill a glass or ask a question. It did nothing to lighten her mood or even his. He found himself wondering what she must be struggling with. He noticed that she didn't have a ring on her finger, so she wasn't married. Maybe she was having problems with her boyfriend.

She came one last time to bring the bill. "Thank you for coming. We'll look forward to seeing you soon," she said mechanically. Once more, the words were appropriate but detached and lifeless.

James reached for the tab, but Troy quickly grabbed it.

"I have this, old boy. Sarah told me about your heroic act with the budget at work. You never cease to amaze me, James. I'm proud to know you."

James's mind knew it was a compliment and that Troy was genuine, but it was a deflating blow to James's pride, which had been fragile all day anyway. Troy knew he had taken a pay cut, and paying the bill, as kind a gesture as it was, hurt. Troy obviously thought James was unable to pay for a basic meal.

As Troy fumbled with the bill and his wallet, James started to thoughtlessly doodle on the napkin with his pen. He thought about his day and knew he needed to get out of this depressed rut he was stuck in. This mood wasn't normal for him. He deserved better; Molly, Troy, and the kids did too. He needed to snap out of it. He heard his mom's voice in his head saying as she had so many times, "The best way to feel better about yourself is to help someone else." He thought about the cash he had in his wallet. On their strict budget, Molly had suggested they use cash so that once it was gone, they knew the budget was gone until the next payday. That way they were not eating into their savings for needless items. The money he had left was for his lunches over the next few weeks.

He looked over and saw Shamanda helping the people at the next table. On impulse he pulled out his wallet, placed the forty-five dollars he had in cash under the folded napkin, and wrote the first thing that came to his mind: "You make a difference. Hope your day gets better."

He knew that Troy would leave a tip too, but the act of

paying Shamanda a tip was, in its own way, liberating. He was proving to himself that he was not completely helpless, that he could help someone else.

As they stood up and made their way to the Diner doors, Troy said nonchalantly, "One more thing. At the end of this week, work is giving me some type of award. They're having a large banquet to celebrate, and Sarah and I would like to have you and Molly join us as our guests."

They stopped in the foyer of the Diner, and James leaned slightly against the double door to steady himself. Troy was getting another award to add to the large collection he must have already.

He really was a success. He was everything that James wasn't. Everything that James wished he could be. Troy wouldn't have any anxiety on *his* fortieth birthday.

4

James Smith

James was back in his office. He didn't remember anything about the walk back from the Diner. The request from Troy had thrown him off.

"What is wrong with me?" he said to the empty room.

That was the big question. Truly, what *was* wrong with him? Why wasn't he as successful or as perfect as Troy—or anyone else for that matter? Why did he feel like he needed to be something else? His life was, in fact, not that bad. He had a beautiful wife and three wonderful children. Where were these unwelcome emotions coming from? Yet, at the same time, James couldn't help but think, *I'm just an accountant, a profession that's so common people's eyes glaze over after they ask me what I do for a living. Nobody awards the accountant. Nobody.*

James sat dejectedly in his chair. *Is this some sort of midlife crisis?* Why couldn't he shake it off and hold on to the happiness he felt at moments throughout the day? There were so many to choose from—with the kids, or Molly, or with Hal and Enric at the office. Why were these moments so fleeting and the discouragement so enduring?

The phone rang. Absentmindedly, he picked it up. "Yes?"

"Lanie is on line three." It was Betty.

"Put her through. Thank you." Lanie was James's younger sister. He was the third of five children, and she was number four. They were born a year apart and shared the brutal reality of being middle children. They were neither the celebrated older siblings nor the spoiled youngest. This unchangeable reality and their closeness in age had forged a strong lasting friendship between Lanie and James. They tried to talk over the phone every few days to stay in touch.

He listened for the click that signaled Betty had connected the lines and said, "Hey, Lane. How're you doing?"

"I'm all right. Camry just threw up carrots all over the rug in the living room." James could hear the dry humor in Lanie's voice. She was always able to use humor to make a stressful situation less tense.

"Sounds like a smelly situation," James joked. "How's Dan?" Lanie and her husband, Dan, had moved to Arizona for work a year ago. Their mother insisted on it being a "horrible idea because . . . think of all the *bad* people in California." As far as either of them knew, their mother had never been to California. Lanie had pointed that out to her once, along with the fact that Arizona and California were different states, and it only resulted in her mother breaking down into tears.

"Dan is really liking the work here." James knew his sister well enough to know that what she said was sometimes less important than what she didn't say. The way she answered his question and avoided talking about herself let James know that Lanie was having a hard time being in Arizona. Despite her adventurous nature, her love for her husband, and the fortitude to prove their mother wrong, the move to Arizona had been hard on Lanie. Camry was their first child, and not being around family when all those "what if" questions arose was a struggle.

He knew this call was a time for him to listen. Lanie would close off if he asked her directly what was wrong, so he had to dance around the subject until he struck a nerve close enough for her to spill it all. James thought of the waitress at the Diner again. It would be nice to focus on helping someone else instead of wallowing in his own worries.

"Good. I'm glad he's liking it. How's the weather?" James figured that was a safe starting point. The weather is only a hot topic with a bride on her wedding day when the rain clouds are gathering.

"It's actually been really nice."

"Have you taken Camry out for a walk on the lake path yet?"

"Not yet. Camry has not been feeling well at all. I don't dare take her out."

"That's too bad. What do you think is bothering her—allergies?"

"I'm not sure. Maybe she's just getting used to the real food. Dan says she's fine, but how would he know? He's not home long enough to see her sick." James knew he had struck the nerve he was fishing for. Lanie was homesick and lonely, and she somehow resented that Dan was at work.

"What do you mean?" He left the question open ended for Lanie to decide if he was talking about Camry or Dan.

"I mean, I'm home all day with Camry and all I ask is that he's home on time for dinner, but the last few days he's come home late every night."

"Why does he say he's late?"

"Work. He has some big project or something." He could hear Lanie's voice shake as she spoke.

"Lane," James said, trying to be as gentle as possible, "he probably does have a project."

"I know. But what if this is only the start? What if he starts coming home later and later until one day he doesn't come home at all?" She was working herself into a frenzy.

"Lanie! What are you talking about? That's not going to happen, and you know it. You're just missing him. Give him a week to finish his project and life will go back to normal. You need to take Camry out for a walk or something so that you aren't home conjuring up things to worry about. Have you been able to get some sleep lately?" He knew that with Molly the times she was the most frenzied were when she was not sleeping well with a new baby in the home.

"No, not much lately. And I know you're right. I just miss him. I miss all of you." Her voice sounded sad.

"I know, Lane, but it's all worth it. Just think, in a few more months Camry will be sleeping through the night, Dan will be done with whatever project he was working on, and life will be normal again." Then, for comic relief, he said, "Go get you some friends!" They both started to laugh.

"Thanks, James. I knew you would help me feel better. I get kind of hysterical sometimes."

"Anytime, Lane. Stress gets to the best of us." *You have no idea*, he thought. "Now, I need to go or I'll be late for the ball game."

"Oh, yes, good luck! Let me know how it goes. Tell Molly hello for me."

James rushed out of his office door and almost bowled Betty over as she stood right outside. "Sorry, Betty! What're you doing?"

"What am I doing?" she asked, her face disbelieving at his absurd question. "What are *you* doing? You're going to be late! That team of yours needs a coach!" She handed him the baby-blue cap that said "Near World" on it.

Betty was stern about most things that James did. She never let much get past her careful eye and was not afraid to point out flaws. However, she was extremely proud of him for coaching a baseball team. She had even been the one to send emails to Mr. Barnes about the team needing a sponsor. Mr. Barnes, of course, accepted because, after all, there would be fifteen children on the field as living advertisements.

"Thanks, Betty."

"Now, go on and get us a win! No time for getting sentimental. It's game time!" She pushed him on the shoulder and shooed him out the door like an unwanted alley cat.

When James arrived at the field, there were only thirty minutes before first pitch. He could see his eclectic group of players wearing their baby-blue uniforms scattered around the field. He didn't have time to change, so he pulled off his tie, put his Near World T-shirt over his collared work shirt, and shoved Betty's cap onto his head.

The game went as all the games did. James alternated between yelling excitedly and praying that the team would succeed. In the seventh, and last, inning, the score was three to one. Near World had a runner on third and a runner who had just stolen from first to second. They could tie the game right here. Maybe even pull ahead.

James looked up at the scoreboard and saw that there were two outs already. He frowned. They would only have one chance. *But one chance is all we need*, James thought, his heart surging with hope. They could do this. They could get a win for him to talk about next time he saw Troy. He turned to see who was up to bat next. He hoped it was one of the team's older players, who was sure to get a hit.

All the hope he had fell to the dirt and shattered when he saw Lucas Tobin, their youngest and smallest player, standing there. Lucas came as a duo with his older brother Ian, who was Jaden's classmate and friend. Ian was a taller, more mature version of Lucas. Lucas, for his part, was just old enough to be included in the league this year. Ian, Jaden, or any of the older players could've handled this situation without a problem. However, James had taken out an older player and put in Lucas an inning earlier so he could get some playing time. James felt a twinge of regret for that decision. Little did he know at the time the swap would be so crucial.

He could sub in someone right now before it was too late. The rule was that a player had to complete an inning before being substituted once in the game. Lucas had played the entire sixth inning. He also had not stepped up to the plate, an important fact since a player could still be switched out before they stepped up to bat.

Making the decision, James stepped toward home plate, ready to call time out for the substitution. However, as he did so, he saw little Lucas pick up his bat and walk to the plate with determination.

The last thing Lucas did was look into the stands. James followed his gaze, and among all the fans he spotted Ian and Lucas's mother, Selma Tobin. Selma waved encouragingly to her youngest son. James stopped in his tracks. He couldn't take Lucas out. He knew it. It would destroy the kid's courage and pride. James turned around and walked back to the third base coaching position, knowing full well he was risking the win with each step.

The first pitch came in fast. Fear in Lucas's eyes paralyzed him. Before he had even started to swing, the umpire yelled "Strike!" James felt the collective groan from the crowd. They too knew what was at stake here.

"It's all right, Luke! You can do it! Just like at practice," James yelled encouragingly.

James had worked hard with Lucas and the two other young kids on the team, trying to help them get over their fear of swinging at a pitched ball instead of a T-ball. They had the habit of jumping out of the way, and he had resorted to placing six bats on the ground behind their feet so they couldn't back out of the batter's box without slipping and falling. Their only choice was to hit the ball or jump forward and *be* hit by the ball. At least Lucas had not jumped backward. Hearing James's encouragement, Lucas once again stepped into the box. His little hands gripped the bat tensely, and the helmet, too large for his head, tilted to the side.

James held his breath as the pitcher wound up and threw another pitch. It was high and outside, an obvious ball, but Lucas swung with all his might. He missed. "Strike two!" the umpire announced.

"That's all right. Good swing, Luke. You're all right. This next pitch is yours."

The pitcher wound up again, and this time Lucas swung and the bat connected with the ball. It was a soft grounder to the second baseman. James's adrenaline surged, and he started jumping up and down screaming, "Go! Go! Go!" The two players on second and third started rounding the bases to home, but James barely noticed. His eyes were on the little legs racing to first base.

The second baseman was distracted momentarily by the runners and didn't know which way to throw the ball. It was only a moment, but it was just enough for Lucas to get a head start. By the time the second baseman turned to throw the ball, Lucas was well on his way to first. James had started to run too. He was cheering on Lucas with all the energy he had.

The ball soared threw the air and was caught by the first basemen moments before Lucas stepped on the base.

"Out!" the first-base umpire called.

James fell to his knees in the dirt. He saw Lucas round the base and watched the euphoria drain from his face as he realized he hadn't made it. The other team ran off the field with excited whoops. Lucas hung his head and started slowly back to the dugout. It broke James's heart to see the boy so discouraged.

James stood up, brushed his suit pants quickly, and walked out to meet Lucas. When he arrived, he saw tears coming down the little boy's face. James knelt again in the dirt so he could look Lucas in the eye.

"You had a great hit, big guy," James said.

"I'm no good." The voice was quiet and full of emotion.

James's own tears stung his eyes. He pulled the little quivering body to his own.

"You are too. You did the very best you could, and that's what matters. I'm so proud of you." He couldn't stop his own tears from falling any longer.

It had been a long day.

5

Shamanda Holley

The lights from the stately porch chased the darkness away from a light-blue Victorian house in Lake Claire, Georgia, just outside of Atlanta. The soft, golden glow spread like the warmth of a hot shower on a cold day until it lit the spacious yard. This view made the long drive worth it.

Shamanda exhaled in relief. She loved this home. So many memories growing up took place here at Grandma Mertyl's. Shamanda realized they referred to it as "Grandma Mertyl's" even though Grandpa Roy still lived here too. She briefly wondered why, but no explanation came, so she turned off her car lights and stepped out. She breathed in the warm dampness of the night air. The locusts and other insects were chirping in a flamboyant night chorus.

The entire family would be waiting for her arrival. She had driven for fifteen hours straight to be here, and it felt so good to be in the South again. She knew she was home when the restaurant she stopped at for lunch asked if she would like sweet tea. She never liked sweet tea much, but she'd ordered some anyway out of sentiment.

Shamanda walked up to the porch. The old wooden double swing was still there. She and her cousins had spent hours entertaining themselves on that swing. She opened the dark oak door, and all of her senses were put on overdrive. *Home.*

The smell of fried food and fresh dinner rolls combined with the chaos of screaming children and the voices of the adults they belonged to. This was her family.

It had been way too long. She missed this. As she stepped into the room, she avoided the creaky floorboard under the homemade welcome mat. The creak had been that way for as long as she remembered—as kids they used to stand on opposite sides of the board and jump, trying to play music.

Shamanda looked up and saw that the large oak-trimmed hall ahead was still offset by the soft yellow paisley wallpaper that had been popular so many years ago. Nobody had noticed her yet. She was content to just soak up the experience of being home for a minute. Seven years of school, a bachelor's degree, and then law school had not left many opportunities to be here with the family. She walked slowly past the large staircase and traced the eclectic family photos with her finger as she absentmindedly made her way to the bright lighting of the kitchen. The faces of several generations smiled back at her from the photos—yes, she was home.

Shamanda walked around the corner to see her family putting final touches on the dinner. "Shey, dear!" Grandma Mertyl's voice calling her by her nickname carried over the din. "Welcome home!" The room stopped. A disbelieving silence pervaded for a few seconds as the family turned to see if it was truly her or just a ghost.

Shamanda felt a bit out of place for a fleeting second. Then Uncle Len piped up, "The favorite has returned!" A wave of voices and hugs welcomed Shamanda into the room.

"Honey, I'm so glad you made it. I was worried." Shamanda's mother latched onto her arm and led her to a chair near the center island. "Did you have a nice drive? Your father told me not to worry, but I always worry about you, dear."

"I'm fine, Mom. Thank you. It's so great to be home." Her mother always worried way too much, and having Shamanda away for school had increased her anxieties. The result was a long list of questions and prodding when she first returned until her mother was satisfied that she was perfectly healthy.

As they sat around the banquet table that spanned the dining room, Shamanda watched the melee with a light heart. This was completely different from her apartment in the city where she lived alone.

Normally, Grandma Mertyl's dining room table appeared to be a monstrous piece that filled the room. However, today, delicious Southern cooking filled the table—city people in the north just didn't know what they were missing. Shamanda looked around at all the faces she loved.

Grandpa Roy stood up. "Heh, hum," he said, clearing his throat. He was always the mildest member of the family. Shamanda smiled because only a few family members had even heard him. He tried again. "Hey, everybody. Let's thank the Lord for our food and especially"—he turned and nodded lovingly toward Shamanda—"for letting our shining star come home."

Warmth spread through Shamanda's whole body. It tingled her skin, and she felt a few tears building up. "Leonard, will you pray for us?" Grandpa sat back down.

Uncle Len stood up. "Let us pray."

Shamanda watched as all of her family reached over and held the hand of the person next to them. They all bowed their heads, even the children. Being a traditional Southern family, Grandma and Grandpa had raised them all to be religious. Stories of faith and love abounded in the Holley household. Again Shamanda felt emotional with gratitude.

As soon as the prayer was finished, the loud craziness started once again. Shamanda dug in, enjoying all that she had missed over the last few years.

After dinner the family had all helped clean up, and then found areas around the house to talk and catch up. Shamanda found herself laughing more than she had in a long time. It was a dream.

Something touched Shamanda's leg. She looked down and saw her five-year-old niece, Alayna. "Hey there, Princess!" Shamanda pulled the small frame up on her lap. Alayna had two perfect dimples, and her mocha skin was the perfect shade with her violet T-shirt. "How are you doing?"

"I's fine."

"You are?" Shamanda teased and tickled Alayna's leg. Alayna laughed, and to Shamanda that sound was perfect.

Alayna became serious again and looked Shamanda in the eye, "Mommy says that I'm like you."

"She does, does she?" Shamanda smiled to think her sister would have said that. They had been close, but not best friends as their mother wished them to be.

Alayna nodded her head, and her two curly pigtails bobbed. "Uh-huh! And she says if I's good, I can be smart as you. And someday I can be a lay-er too." Alayna's Southern drawl pulled on the vowels as she said "lawyer."

Alayna's words shattered Shamanda's feelings of dreamy comfort. Reality returned, hard. Thankfully, Alayna jumped off her lap and ran to join the other children.

All the words that had brought Shamanda joy earlier were now replaying in her head, and this time they brought despair. "Our favorite . . . Our shining star . . ." They, her entire family, thought she was something that she wasn't.

She was a counterfeit.

6

Shamanda Holley

It was well past midnight when Shamanda parked her used Nissan sedan in the parking lot near her apartment. The complex was run down and sad. The trash and peeling vinyl siding gave the entire complex a depressed and unclean feeling. But this was where Shamanda called home. It was a far cry from the Victorian family home in Lake Claire.

Shamanda pushed open the door and stretched her achy legs. It had been a long drive back. She had enjoyed the time with the family, but the whole weekend she couldn't shake the feeling that she was putting up a front for them all to see—the faux Shamanda. She was trying to live up to the person they thought she was, but she was failing miserably.

Thinking of little Alayna's sweet face, Shamanda walked briskly from her car to her studio. Even after five years of living here she still did not feel comfortable outside by herself at night. The loud, hectic noise from the overcrowded apartments filled the courtyard. There were a few dim lights in the area, but they only accentuated the hazy shadows and, in Shamanda's opinion, only made it worse. Very different from the world she had just left in Georgia, on so many levels.

She thought of Alayna, along with the rest of the family, believing that Shamanda was successful and wonderful. Someday, Alayna would find out the truth, just like being told after years of believing and hoping that there was no reality behind the miracles of Santa Claus and the Easter Bunny. Someday Alayna would know that Shamanda was a failure.

Shamanda fumbled with the keys to the dingy door and stepped inside. Something crinkled under her feet. She put down the bags she carried and flipped on the light switch. It sputtered for a moment and then hummed to life. She looked down to see three days' worth of mail.

Shamanda picked the letters up and thumbed through them. A moment later, she wished she hadn't.

The first was a letter from the law firm she had interviewed with last week, the golden embossing standing out on the heavy paper. The beautiful letter, however, couldn't hide the rejection that boiled down to four ugly words: "We chose someone else." Of course the letter said other things, just like all the other letters she had received. Yet they all had the same result: rejection.

It had been nearly six months since Shamanda had graduated from law school and passed the bar exam. But she still couldn't find a job. She was trying, but nothing was working out. She could fill out the application forms in her sleep now, but there always seemed to be someone smarter or more qualified than her, or from an Ivy League school, and they landed the job.

She tossed the letter on the table where there was a stack of older rejection letters already. Shamanda had begun to call it her "paper cemetery."

The next letter was from the bank that held her student loan. Shamanda skimmed the formal first few sentences, and then her heart sank when she read, "Your six month moratorium is nearly expired. You will need to make your first student loan payment on the 30th of this month."

With that letter, Shamanda's day became worse.

She was already struggling to pay the rent on her dirty studio; now she needed to start paying her student loans too. Shamanda was too proud to ask for help from family. By doing that, she would have to expose her secret failure, and she couldn't bear to see her family disappointed. They had all sacrificed so much to help her be here already.

Already depressed, she opened the next letter. Inside was another letter from a lawyer's office that she hadn't applied to. Shamanda skimmed it and was thankful this letter was not a rejection letter. Then one word made Shamanda nearly stop breathing: eviction.

Shamanda dropped the rest of the letters and sat slowly on the bed. Her eyes started to water. She wiped quickly at the tears, took a few breaths, and started to read.

The letter outlined that she would be evicted next week if she didn't make a payment soon. Homeless? She had a law degree and was facing a future without a home.

Exhausted, Shamanda sprawled backward onto the bed. She stared at the ugly popcorn ceiling she had stared at every stressful night of law school. She used to refer to it as the "hideous ceiling" and couldn't wait to never see it again. Now she realized it was better than no ceiling at all.

It wasn't supposed to be like this. She had believed in her dreamy fairy-tale life too. She'd had it all planned out. She would graduate from high school, get a bachelor's, become a lawyer, and save the world. She had kept a mental checklist and found satisfaction crossing off each of those milestones as she completed them. She couldn't save the world without a job. *This isn't part of the plan*, she thought in desperation.

Shamanda thought of the big, loving family she'd left back in Atlanta. What would they think of her when they found out that she wasn't working as a lawyer but as a waitress for lawyers? Shamanda groaned in pain. One tear escaped her eye, and she felt it trace down her cheekbone and onto her ear. She saw her mother's face, so full of love, and the wave of tears couldn't be stopped.

Finally, when Shamanda's eyes were hurting and dry and her sleeve was soaked, she stood up and walked to the bathroom. She splashed cold water on her face and looked up as she dried off the remaining water.

She stared at herself and suddenly heard Grandma Mertyl's calming voice in her head: "Honey, we will always love you. You gotta have faith."

It was something she had heard her Grandma say for years whenever they were having a hard time. "I'm trying, Grandma, but it's so hard," Shamanda said out loud.

She knew that her Grandma would have waved away Shamanda's protests of how hard it was and repeated, "The Lord will help, but you gotta have faith."

Shamanda smiled and said to herself, "Okay, Grandma, I'll try."

7

Shamanda Holley

Thud. Thud. Thud.

Shamanda opened her eyes. They were stinging and puffy from last night's cry. She rolled over and looked at the clock: seven o'clock. Her alarm hadn't even gone off yet. She was hoping to sleep in today, at least for a few minutes. Yesterday had been a long, draining day.

Thud. Thud.

That noise was coming from the hallway. Shamanda sighed and rolled over. The neighbors must be doing something already. "Can't you just wait until nine?" Shamanda grumbled to herself and rolled away from the morning light streaming in from the window.

Thud. "Miss Holley?" *Thud. Thud.*

Shamanda's eyes shot open. That thud was the front door and someone had just called her by name. She jumped out of bed and threw on an old T-shirt and the pants from the night before.

"Coming." She had no idea who would be here this early in the morning. She opened the door, squinted at the light, and saw a man in a suit.

"Miss Holley?" he asked, his voice formal and unfriendly.

"Yes?"

"I am here to hand-deliver an eviction notice." Shamanda grasped the door and leaned into it for support. It took all her control not to fall over or cry—or both. She nodded as the man continued to talk. She was in overwhelmed mode and could only register that he was giving her documents and asking her to sign that she had received them.

Shamanda shut the door and put the notice on the cemetery pile. Her life was becoming a nightmare.

Rent was due. She was one month late because it had been a hard month. She needed the money for daily living. She was planning on making up the payments this month, but that wasn't pulling together either. The landlord was keen on getting her out of the unit because her lease was not up for several months, and he couldn't raise the rent until then—or until he kicked her out.

Shamanda calculated in her head as she showered for work. Rent was 275 dollars a month. For two months' rent, she would need 550 dollars. She dried her hair and walked to the chest of drawers. Reaching way back in the top drawer, she pulled out her stash of money. She counted it, and the total was two hundred and eighty dollars. This was the money from work that she hadn't yet deposited at the bank.

Sitting down on the bed, Shamanda opened her laptop and signed in to her bank account. The balance was two hundred and ten. Her total amount was four hundred and ninety. That was it. She had nothing else. That money was needed to pay for rent, food, gas, electricity—everything. If she paid it all to rent, she wouldn't be able to eat. Or drive.

A surge of hope sprung up when she thought maybe

the landlord would accept a large partial payment. She walked over to the paper cemetery and picked up the eviction notice again. Her hope was dashed again; big red letters at the bottom the paper read: TO AVOID EVICTION AMOUNT NEEDS TO BE PAID IN FULL. She needed to make up the difference.

The money from her dad! She had forgotten about it. Shamanda dug into her pocket. Last night before she left Georgia, her dad had handed her some cash. Initially, she had refused because she knew they didn't have much to spare either, but inwardly she was so thankful he had offered it. He had told her to "get something nice to eat for dinner on your way back." Shamanda just kept the money and didn't eat, and now she was glad she had made that decision.

Unrolling the crumpled bills, Shamanda let out a sigh of relief. Her father had given her two twenty-dollar bills. Shaking with emotion she smoothed out the bills as if they were plated with gold. That brought her total up to five hundred and ten dollars. She wasn't there yet, but she was closer. "Thank you, Daddy. Thank you."

Shamanda put on the yellow Diner outfit, which she hated. She looked in the mirror and felt like a combination of a nurse out of a 1950s movie and a yellow starburst. She pinned on her white plastic name tag. She had started working at the Diner during law school because the hours were great for working around her school schedule. She had never dreamed that it would become her sole source of income for so long.

All day Shamanda served men and women dressed in suits who were discussing business. They treated her as someone less than them, someone without an education. All she was good for was to fill their drinks and clear their tables. Little did they know that she had an equal or higher education level than most of them. Sometimes Shamanda would linger a bit longer than she needed just to hear their conversations. It made her feel like she was learning still.

Shamanda put on some eyeliner and mascara, hopefully masking her cried-out eyes. She knew that she needed to make forty dollars today to break even. She did the math. Forty dollars was approximately twenty tables. Most eaters at the Diner only paid two dollars for tip. On an average day Shamanda had fifteen to seventeen tables. Twenty would be pushing it.

"Okay, Grandma. I'm having faith here. I just need twenty tables today."

She knew the car was on empty, so Shamanda decided to ride the subway to work. She packed her running shoes in a bag because she knew her commuting card only had enough money for one trip. She would have to walk home.

Shamanda grabbed her keys and purse and headed out the door, leaving her paper cemetery behind her. Hopefully this would work out.

8

Shamanda Holley

Shamanda walked into the Diner from the back door for employees. The familiar smells of work—oil, coffee, and pancake batter—overwhelmed her. This was the same smell that Shamanda felt like she emanated at the end of her shift. Shamanda hung up her purse on the hooks next to the door.

"Twenty tables . . . twenty tables," she told herself over and over as she began her morning process. Customers would show up in a few hours, and she wanted to be ready. She *had* to make money today. It was either that or become homeless.

The Diner doors jingled, and Shamanda looked up; it was the first wave of customers. She grabbed a few menus, greeted the two men, and guided them to a table. She handed them the menus, hoping they would order breakfast. In the morning several people came in just for coffee, and although it was nice not to have to worry about them as much, they usually left horrible tips if they left any at all.

"How does this work for you?" Shamanda gave them a booth near the exterior wall.

"That is great. Thank you." The men slid into the seats, and Shamanda handed them the menus. One of the men dismissed the menus with his hand. "Only coffee, please."

Disheartened, Shamanda brought them their coffee. Today was not turning out the way she wanted it to. Now she needed to have twenty-one tables.

Two more tables came in. One was another "coffee only," and she had to give the next table to Jami, the other waitress this morning, who had just come in to start her shift too. Shamanda ended the first two hours of work by collecting a grand total of one dollar and twenty-five cents in tips. The next hour was extremely slow. She and Jami even had time to do things they usually didn't do, like switch out and wash all the salt and pepper shakers on the tables.

"Shamanda?" her boss called to her. Shamanda had been concentrating on not spilling any salt and jumped when he called her name.

"Yeah?" she answered, brushing salt off the table.

"It looks like it is going to be a slow day. Since you came in early, you can go after the lunch rush. Jami can finish up the shift."

Shamanda's mind reeled. *This cannot be happening!* She was fighting a losing battle. She had been working all day and had only made about seven dollars—not even close to the forty dollars she needed. All she could say was, "Okay." It came out as a croak. If she attempted to say anything else, she might break down right there. She couldn't risk being sent home even earlier.

The lunch "rush" was anything but. Four or five more tables came in, and Shamanda and Jami split them. The reality of her situation was weighing heavily as the time passed, and her pocket was still mostly empty.

"This one is yours." Jami elbowed Shamanda as they finished up the salt and pepper shakers. Shamanda looked up to see, yet again, another man in a business suit walk into the Diner. She wiped her hands and took a menu to meet him. He was scanning the room as if looking for someone.

"Hello, can I help you?" She walked toward him.

The guy looked around the room one more time before settling on Shamanda's face. "Oh, I'm meeting a friend for lunch. He must not be here yet."

"All right, let's find you a table while you're waiting." Shamanda showed him to a booth and laid two menus on the table. "Can I get you a cup of coffee?"

"No, thank you. A glass of water is fine."

Shamanda walked away. Water? A glass of water? That was the only thing worse than a cup of coffee. Water didn't even cost anything. Today was not the day to try to have faith. Shamanda filled a glass with ice and started to fill the water. "Sorry, Grandma. It's not working out."

"What?" Jami asked as she picked up the food for her table from the kitchen window.

Shamanda hadn't realized she'd said that out loud. "Oh, nothing. I was just talking to myself."

She walked over and placed the water in front of the man, who was obviously distracted. He had an eye trained on the Diner door.

Shamanda started to clear off some other tables and get ready to leave for the day. She looked up and saw that another man had entered, and the distracted man at the table stood up to hug him. Shamanda wiped the table one more time and dropped off the plates for the dishwasher. She made her way over to the two men, now deep in conversation.

"Are you two ready to order? Or do you need a minute?" she interrupted.

"I'm ready. You ready?" the distracted man mumbled without looking up from his menu.

"All right, what can I get for you? My name is Shamanda, I will be helping you today." Shamanda pulled out her pad of paper and a pen to take their order. This could very well be the last order of the day. All Shamanda wanted to do was go home and be alone.

The distracted man finally closed his menu and looked up with a smile. "Hello, Shamanda. How are you today?" The question and the smile felt genuine, especially from a man that seemed so distracted earlier. Most people didn't look up as they ordered. Shamanda didn't know what to say. She was tempted to tell him the truth for a second. Then she recalled that he was only a customer, and he didn't really mean it. He was asking a polite question to evoke a polite answer.

"I'm all right. Thank you for asking," Shamanda forced herself to answer and smile, both of which felt far from the truth.

"Well, in that case, I'll have the daily special." Again he smiled and then turned to the other man.

This was the first time Shamanda had seen the other man's face. They looked about the same age, but this man looked stressed. He looked up and held out his menu for Shamanda to take. "Make that two. Thank you, Shamanda." Shamanda wrote down the order and took the menu. She was sure that he never even looked at it before he ordered, but she had her own problems to worry about. Shamanda left them to place the order.

Shamanda went back a few times to check on the men. The second guy always called her by name and made sure to thank her for even filling their glasses. At this point the Diner was starting to have fewer and fewer people. The lunch rush, if you could call it that, was over. The thought was sad to Shamanda. She had hoped Grandma Mertyl was right, but it was looking less and less likely.

She just needed to get these two men out of the Diner so she could start her walk home. She could sleep on her bed for at least a few more nights.

Shamanda took the bill over to them. "Thank you for coming. We'll look forward to seeing you soon." She picked up a few of their dishes and went back to clean up.

As she passed one of Jami's tables, an older lady in the booth stopped her. "Miss, can I have some tea?"

"Sure you can." The woman reminded her of Grandma Mertyl. She brought the tea back to the older couple and saw that the men were finally leaving. She went over to clean up their dishes.

She looked at the bill and saw that the man had left a five-dollar tip. That was more than average, but it still only brought her daily total up to twenty-one dollars. She was close. But the red ink from the eviction notice—"PAID IN FULL"—burned in her mind.

Shamanda fought tears as she cleared the remaining items on the table. There wasn't much left, so she also collected the paper goods. She noticed that one of the napkins had writing on it. She set down a plate and picked up the napkin to read what it said. She was expecting to see some kind of business plan or meeting notes. She was surprised to read the words, "You make a difference. Hope your day gets better."

As Shamanda brought it closer, the napkin unfolded and money fell out. Shamanda looked up to see if the men were still in the Diner. They were gone. With shaking hands she picked up the cash. She counted it. Forty-five dollars—what she needed plus some. Combined with the twenty-one dollars she had made earlier, she would have some money left over after she paid her rent and put gas in the car.

Shamanda left work with a heart full of gratitude.

"Thank you, Grandma, for challenging me to have faith. And thank you, Lord, for not giving up on me." Tears of joy flowed freely as Shamanda spoke the words. For the first time in several days, she felt hope.

She then thought of the man who was willing to help her without even knowing why or what she needed help with. His money may have been pocket change to him, but to her, forty-five dollars meant the world. "Lord, bless the kind man in the suit. You know who he is; bless him for being an angel in my life."

Shamanda hoped that one day she would meet the kind man in the suit again. She wished she had paid more attention to what he looked like. She would just have to trust that someone, somewhere, would let that man know how much of a difference he made in people's lives.

9

Shamanda Holley

All night Shamanda was in awe of the blessing that had taken place in her life. Every few hours she would open her wallet to see the money, just to make sure it was real. Against all her instincts and analytical training as a lawyer, she had trusted in God and leaned on the faith of her family, and what had happened could only be described as a miracle.

There was no other way to explain it. How else would the businessman know to leave extra money? A few times, logic fought back the idea of a faith-based answer, and she wondered if the money was left by mistake. Then she would reread the note written on the Diner napkin sitting ceremoniously on her table, and she knew it wasn't an accident. Her prayers had been answered.

She wanted to share the joy she was feeling with someone. But who? She knew the person who would love to hear the story the most was Grandma Mertyl, but telling her family about the miracle would force her to be honest about her entire situation.

Suddenly the thought of being truthful with her family wasn't so daunting. Shamanda actually felt it was time for her to be honest with them. The more she thought about it, the more she felt comforted by the idea.

Before she could change her mind, Shamanda dug through her purse for her cell phone, and for the second time in a day she went against her judgment and took a leap of faith.

She dialed her parent's number and heard her dad's deep voice. "Is this my little girl calling? Do you miss us already?"

Shamanda had a lump of emotions lodged in her throat. "Hi, Daddy," she finally said with a shaky voice.

"Are you all right? What happened? Are you hurt?" Her father had heard her emotions and was on alert already.

Shamanda sniffed and took a deep breath. "I'm all right, Dad. But I need to talk to you."

"Go ahead, baby. You know we're always here." Shamanda knew that "we" meant her mom had picked up one of the other phones and was listening in. She smiled through her tears, thankful she knew her parents well enough to predict their actions.

"Hi, Mom."

"Shey, dear, what's the matter?" She heard the unveiled worry in her mother's question.

"I haven't been completely honest with you." That was the hardest sentence to say. But now that it was spoken, there was no turning back. Shamanda continued to talk into the silence, "But I had something happen today that made me realize how important all of you are to me, and I knew I needed to talk about it."

"Go on, baby girl, we're listening," her father coaxed.

Shamanda started to tell them about her situation—all of

it. She told them about not finding a job, about the eviction, about her guilt when she was with all of them, and finally she told them what had happened earlier in the day at the Diner. To her parents' credit, they had listened and cried right along with her.

"Shey, dear, I'm glad you finally told us. I wish you would've said something sooner. Family is here to help each other. We love you, Shamanda."

"I know you do. Thanks for listening."

It was hard for Shamanda to end the conversation, but as she climbed into bed she felt better about life than she had in a long time.

Thud. Thud. Thud.

Shamanda woke up to someone pounding on her door. Panic surged through her. *Who could it be this time?* She wrapped a robe around herself and walked to the door, nervous that it was another messenger of bad news.

She opened the door and saw a friendly man wearing the brown suit of his shipping company. "Are you Ms. Holley?" Shamanda, thankful he wasn't a bill collector or a lawyer, focused and registered that he was handsome. She self-consciously fiddled with her robe, keenly aware of her early-morning disheveled look.

"Yes, I'm Shamanda."

The man smiled and handed her a thick 8×10 express mail envelope. "Have a good day, ma'am." The man smiled again and headed down the stairs.

Shamanda shut the door and looked at the envelope. The neat, unmistakable handwriting on the front was her father's. It had been mailed late in the evening yesterday. She opened the package and inside, wrapped in several layers of paper, was a stack of bills. There was only one short note, this time in Grandma Mertyl's hand. It said, "Sometimes answers to prayers come from unexpected places and through an ordinary delivery person. Even Shining Stars need to wear a yellow Diner uniform once or twice. But that doesn't mean your family doesn't think you are special. We all love you!"

Sudden tears welled up and fell from Shamanda's eyes. She pulled the letter close to her chest and said a prayer of thankfulness. She pictured all of her family collecting what cash they had to send to her. She had never felt more loved in her life than she did in that moment.

10

Troy Walker

T*roy had been* at college for two years now. So far he had suffered through the weekdays for the sake of the weekend parties. College parties, he had discovered, were the perfect place to find girls. He'd thought classes might be another possibility, but so far that hadn't panned out.

"Troy!" Troy turned to see his roommate, James, calling from down the hall of the student center where Troy had just finished lunch with a girl he'd met last night. Troy had spent the entire lunch trying, unsuccessfully, to remember her name. Luckily; he didn't have to think too hard, she gushed the entire time about being with him, and Troy didn't have to talk much. It was all so easy.

Troy stopped and waited for James to catch up. "What's up J-man? I didn't think I would see you here."

"I was just passing through to my next class when I saw you. You were meeting a girl?"

Troy was surprised. "How'd you know that?"

"You're wearing your blue shirt." Troy looked down as if he had forgotten what he was wearing and saw his trusty blue shirt. It was the perfect color for his blue eyes and the perfect material to show off all his work in the gym. Vain? A bit, but it worked when trying to get a date—every time.

"Why do you act surprised? I've roomed with you for two years now; I know your tricks. I'm actually surprised all the girls on campus haven't caught on," James teased and started to walk.

Troy stepped up to walk beside him. James asked, "Who was she, by the way? Anyone I know?"

Troy wasn't sure what to say. James didn't miss the hesitation and started to laugh out loud. "You don't even know her name! You're despicable."

"I tried to remember, but I couldn't." Troy tried to sound contrite.

"Man, you're bound to get yourself into a big problem at some point. But I didn't want to talk to you about your dating life. I actually was going to ask you if you were still planning on playing in the game tonight."

James and Troy had formed a team in the college intramural touch football league. Their team had done really well over the years. Both James and Troy enjoyed getting out and using up some energy.

"Of course, old boy. I wouldn't miss it. I may not remember some girl's name, but I wouldn't forget our game!"

"You're horrible," James said again with a laugh.

"What?"

James just rolled his eyes in mock disgust and said, "Well, maybe you can get some of your fan club to come cheer for us tonight." Troy watched his roommate walk away and made his way back to their apartment.

Troy's true focus for the last two years had been dating and any kind of sport activity he could try. Class was the last thing he was worried about. Troy couldn't find any reason to be in his classes other than to sleep, and he could do that at home, so most of the time he just didn't go.

"Hey, Troy, do you have a minute?" For the second time this morning someone called his name. He turned around and saw his math professor, Dr. Yarkov, who was as harsh as the sound of his name. He was stout and wore a full beard that blended into his bushy eyebrows.

"Sure, Doc! What can I do for you?"

Yarkov sneered at Troy's familiarity. "Actually, I noticed that you passed your test."

"I guess I did. Thanks for the congrats."

"I wasn't congratulating you. In fact, it's quite the opposite. I have also noticed you sleep in my class most of the days you come. I'd rather not have you disturbing my students."

"Right. Thanks, Yarkov." Troy knew what Dr. Yarkov was really saying. Just like all his other professors, they had an unspoken understanding. He didn't come and disturb the class with his sleeping, and they gave him the grade he deserved from passing the tests. It was what Troy called a symbiotic relationship.

However, Troy couldn't deny that this third year had not been as easy as the first two. General education classes were easier to breeze through, and he'd found his grades were suffering this year.

As promised, Troy called several of the girls he had numbers for and asked them to come support the game. He was happy that even James was impressed with the squealing ladies in the audience. They won, of course.

A few weeks later, Troy rushed into the house to see if James was there.

He was excited for his plans for the evening, and he wanted to get James involved. The kid was way too serious about his schooling.

"Hey J-man! It's Friday! Want to go out and have some fun?" he called out as he entered the door of their small, sparsely furnished apartment. Most of the furniture had been collected on the side of the road from families moving out of the area. They had a small area with a sink, microwave, and fridge that functioned as their kitchen, and they shared the one bathroom—complete with 1940s pink tiles—and the large bedroom.

Troy found James sitting at his small desk in the corner of the bedroom, writing furiously.

"You're going to kill that paper if you write any harder."

James looked up with a hint of annoyance. "I have a big paper due tomorrow."

"Put it aside, bro. I have some really cute girls lined up tonight, and I can't possibly handle all of them by myself."

"Troy, when are you ever going to realize you can't just play these girls?"

"What are you talking about? Let's go."

Much to Troy's surprise, James didn't respond with the happy response that Troy's invitations usually elicited. James stood up, and mid-stride out of the room he just stared at Troy. Troy tried to understand what James was doing.

"Yo! James? Are you in there? Let's go."

James finally reacted, but not in the way Troy was expecting. His whole body tensed up, and his face flushed with what Troy thought was frustration. Why was he angry?

"Seriously, Troy? You're better than this. You know it. All of your playing around is only leading you toward failure, man," James said.

Now it was Troy's turn to stare silently. Troy had never seen James like this before. James was never upset, let alone at Troy. He stood silently and watched his roommate shake his head nervously as if he too was surprised by his own reaction.

Finally Troy broke the silence. "I was only asking you to come and eat with the girls."

"I know, Troy." Troy could hear the exasperation in James's quiet voice. "It's just hard seeing you throw away all your opportunities. Don't you care at all? You're in a great school. You have talents the rest of us only dream about, and you're wasting them." James stopped and turned to leave the room. As he was closing the door behind him, he said, "You're better than this," without looking back.

James's words echoed in Troy's ears. His stomach knotted up, and suddenly the night out with the girls didn't seem so appealing anymore. James had struck a chord, but Troy couldn't sort through his own thoughts to decipher what chord it was.

A part of him was defensive. Who was James to judge him anyway? He had never asked for his advice in the first place. James was his roommate, not his parent. Yet he couldn't deny that James cared. They had spent plenty of time together over the past two years, and there was one thing Troy knew about James: he was genuine. Was there something to his words? Was Troy wasting his life?

He mindlessly sat down on the kitchen chair next to him. He and James had purchased it from the salvage yard. A few screws were rusted and couldn't be tightened, making the chair a bit wobbly. They had decided the chair had "character," and it had produced plenty of laughs over the years as people sat on it for the first time and promptly jumped up, thinking they had broken it. Once they were initiated, they too would watch the next person experience the terror of nearly falling.

On the table lay Troy's textbooks. He opened the book

on top of the pile—Geometry. He thumbed through the pages, not really looking for anything, and realized that this was the first time he had opened the book since he had bought it three weeks ago. The school bookstore receipt was still in the front cover. He stopped on a page about halfway through and saw a few shapes with angles, symbols, and numbers represented and then broken down into an algorithm. He had no idea how to solve the equation. Having kept the habit of missing classes, he was far behind. No way was he passing this class like he had done with his general education classes.

Troy thought of the scholarship that he had been awarded out of high school. Coming from a small farming town, he graduated with a class of eighty-five people. It wasn't hard competition to be the top of the class academically. He was given the scholarship on that basis. His mother and father had been so happy. Their moderate farm was doing all right to live on, but they never earned enough financially to afford college.

His mother knew this was Troy's chance to get out of what she called the "debt cycle" and become something. They had thrown a huge party to send him off, and the entire town had come out to celebrate. It felt as if everyone was rooting for him the day he left. He was invincible.

Troy knew if he failed his classes this year, he would lose his scholarship. He was already on probation from the previous year. All of a sudden the harsh conversation with James made his situation clearer. James had proven Troy was not invincible after all.

He would fail if he continued on this path.

He had filled his nights and weekends with fun and useless distractions. He pictured the desperation and disappointment on his mother's face if he returned a failure. He could almost feel the silence of disapproval from his father.

He could not let that happen. He could not become a failure.

Troy dug into his pocket and pulled out a crumpled pink paper with a number scrawled across it. He had met the girls at the burger joint on campus. A few months ago he had started a new challenge with himself to see how long it took for girls to give their number up. This girl, a brunette from Florida—he couldn't even remember her name—had not taken long. He stood up from the old chair, walked to the phone on the wall, and dialed.

She picked up after one ring. Momentarily he thought how desperate she must have been. Then he remembered why he had called.

"Hey . . . I'm sorry, but I won't be able to make it tonight. I have a test tomorrow." Those were words he never thought he would say—especially to a girl.

I'm better than this, he thought. He needed to change.

11

Troy Walker

I*t had been* several years since those days with James at college. "I can do the dishes tonight," Troy told Sarah as they finished dinner. He could see that she was a bit frazzled after a long day of chasing children.

Typically, Sundays were bonding days for the family, ones they would spend attending church together or enjoying the warm weather by flying kites or having a picnic. However, both of their children had started to throw up within an hour of each other, and both children seemed to want only their mother.

Troy had busied himself cooking dinner for himself and Sarah. Sarah glanced up with weary eyes. She looked as if she would collapse onto the table and sleep had there not been a plate occupying the space. "Thank you. Thanks for dinner too."

"You were amazing today. I wish that I could've been more help." He felt a surge of affection as he watched his wife get up to check on the kids. He reached out and grabbed her hand as she passed. Her dark hair was tied back into a loose ponytail, strands escaping in all directions. She was still beautiful, even after such a long day. She squeezed his hand back, a silent "I love you," and headed up the stairs.

Troy had married Sarah shortly after they'd graduated from college. After he had turned his college career around, he was a little more specific about whom he dated. Sarah was different than all the other girls. She was smart, witty, and open. She kept him grounded, and most of all she believed in him and encouraged him to become better.

The dishes didn't take long, and Troy found Sarah in their bedroom drying her hair after a shower. He started unloading his pockets, realizing how tired he also felt. He placed his phone on the desk next to his keys, the same place he always did so he could find them easily in the morning. As he did, he noticed the blinking red light that meant he had an unread email. Out of habit he turned his phone on and read it. It was from his assistant, Keith. Keith was young and efficient, and Troy knew a man like him would not be in this position for long; he would move up in the company quickly. The message was short and direct.

"Meeting with R.E. 9 a.m. tomorrow. At his request."

"What?" Troy said incredulously. He reread Keith's email. He looked at the date and time and saw that it had been sent just a few minutes before.

"Everything okay?" Sarah asked, walking lethargically over to him and wrapping her arms around his waist to read the email over his shoulder. Troy was still trying to process it and had barely registered that Sarah was there. "Who is R.E.?" Sarah asked after she read the email.

"Ronald Eckhert. As in Ronald Eckhert of Eckhert Technology," Troy answered, dazed.

"Really?" Sarah's voice echoed in dreamy admiration.

Then she suddenly dropped her arms, and the lethargy was replaced by alarm. "Wait, why does he want to meet with you?"

Troy turned to her and saw the worry creasing her brow. "I don't know. That's what I was wondering."

"Why is he here? Doesn't he live in Los Angeles or something? Does he normally request meetings with people?"

"I'm not sure. I've only seen him one other time, and that was when I went to a regional conference. He's the founder of the company, on a completely different echelon than what I deal with every day."

"Why do you think he wants to meet with you?" Sarah repeated.

"I have no idea."

"Should we be worried?" Sarah's question was almost a whisper, as if she was sharing a secret. Troy stepped over to her and gave her a hug.

"No, I'm sure it's just something about work," he soothed, but he couldn't shake the nervous nagging in the back of his mind. Tomorrow could wind up being a *very* interesting day.

Troy didn't sleep. His mind kept playing Keith's message through his head. He sorted through all kinds of possibilities of why the *big* boss wanted to meet with him. He closed his eyes, but sleep evaded him. "It's probably just to be introduced to a new product," he told himself as he rolled over for the tenth time in the last five minutes. He roughly fluffed his pillow a few times, trying to get comfortable. Or he might be fired the next day. The thought caused him to catch his breath. Not even fluffing the pillow could make that thought go away.

What had he done wrong? He rubbed his burning, tired eyes and listened to Sarah's soft breathing. His mind just wouldn't stop. Troy thought carefully through all recent transactions to see if he had missed something. He also thought of all his employees to see if one of them had a problem. Blank. He was completely clueless as to what to expect when he arrived at work in the morning.

By the time the clock read 4:45, Troy gave up and got out of bed. He put on a blue shirt for luck, a habit from his college days that he had never given up.

The drive to work was just as daunting as sleeping. He couldn't help thinking that this could be his last drive into work, his last time to park in the Eckhert parking lot as an employed person.

Keith was waiting for him at the door as he always was. He looked like he hadn't slept either. His normally starched shirt was a bit wrinkled, and his hair was standing in an odd direction above his right ear where he habitually rubbed his hand when he was working on a frustrating problem. Troy thought that he probably looked that ragged too.

"Did you see my email?" The question was abrupt.

"Good morning to you too. Yes, I saw it. Thank you for ruining my sleep patterns." Troy tried to sound jovial but knew that neither he nor Keith felt it at the moment.

Keith went on as if he hadn't even heard. "I came in early to review some of our last transactions. I paid closer attention to anything over ten thousand dollars because I knew that those were important enough for the big boss to come all the way here. I couldn't find anything. Do you know why he's here?'

It made Troy a little bit relieved to know he was not the only one overthinking the situation, but it also unnerved him to see that Keith also thought there must be a major problem to have Mr. Eckhert here himself. Usually he just sent one of his no-name cronies.

"I'm not sure. We'll find out soon though."

Troy walked in silence with Keith the rest of the way

to the office. Usually they would discuss the day's events and meetings. Today they could only focus on one meeting—like the blaring red fire alarm light on the wall that draws your attention no matter how hard you try to ignore it.

Just as they neared his office door, Troy said, "Hey, Keith, thank you for all your work today. I appreciate it. And you may want to fix your hair before he shows up." Keith nodded and walked toward the bathroom door.

Troy entered his office and shut the door. He sat down in his chair, maybe for the last time. He looked across the room. Next to his office door hung several photos of his family and one plaque with the phrase that had changed his life boldly printed in black: You're Better Than That. If someone didn't know the background, it was an odd statement, but to Troy that phrase meant everything. What James had said that day in college so many years ago had woken Troy up. It had been the first step toward Troy's success today.

Troy's cell phone vibrated with a text message notification. It was Sarah. "Good luck today. You're in my prayers . . . let me know when you're done."

He was just about to type a response when Keith burst into the room. He shut the door behind him. Troy saw that Keith had thrown a suit jacket over his wrinkled shirt, and his hair had been slicked back. It wasn't as perfect as Keith was accustomed to, but it worked.

"Are you ready? He's here. I just had the receptionist show him to the conference room. Or is there another room that you think would be better?" Keith's nerves, coupled with no sleep, were making him frantic.

"No, the conference room is perfect. Thank you, Keith." Troy stood and walked down the hallway. He could feel his coworkers peering around cubicle corners watching him walk to his doom. He wondered flippantly if they would be happy to see him fired. Troy was not naïve enough to think that everyone in the office liked his leadership.

He reached down and took a deep breath before opening the conference room door. As he entered, there was a flurry of activity. Mr. Ronald Eckhert was sitting at the head of the large polished maple table with three of his staff scurrying away with their files. They shuffled out and closed the door. Panic filled Troy as silence ensued.

Mr. Eckhert wore a navy-blue power suit with a bright-red and pale-blue tie. Everything about him screamed *power*, from his shiny wingback shoes to his cuff links and hair gel. Troy hoped he'd have such a healthy head of hair when he was Mr. Eckhert's age.

Mr. Eckhert finally looked up from the paper he was signing and observed Troy standing at the other end of the table. "Come sit down here, son," Mr. Eckhert commanded and waved to a seat near him. "You look like a caged animal. Surely you don't think I bite?" Eckhert emitted a chuckle that sounded more like a snort.

Troy tried to force a laugh, but it ended up sounding more like a choke. He took the seat next to the owner of one of the fastest growing companies in the country and said, "Well, sir, it's not every day you show up in the office. So, yes, I'm a bit nervous." There was something liberating about saying that morsel of truth, even if it did make him appear weak to his boss.

Eckhert burst into hearty laughter that filled the room. Troy was shocked by the response and froze, unsure of how to interpret Mr. Eckhert's reaction.

"They told me that I would like you." Troy wondered who "they" were and how they knew him. "They said you were from a small town and that you were different from our other office directors."

Troy chose not to address the second part of his boss's statement. "Yes sir, I am from a small farming community."

"Well, you wouldn't know that now, would you?" Mr. Eckhert seemed completely in control and was obviously used to having that advantage during a conversation. Troy, on the other hand, couldn't seem to work out where to place his hands. "I guess you're right. I don't usually come unannounced to offices. Actually, I don't get out of that blasted headquarters as much as I want to. Those numbskulls working under me seem to think that if I left the office the place would crumble like a thousand-year-old building in Athens."

Troy stayed quiet, unsure of why he his boss was sharing his personal thoughts.

"The truth is, I wanted to come." He looked Troy right in the eye as if expecting an answer. "They told me that someone else could do it, but I felt that I owed it to you to do it myself. So here I am." Troy's stomach plummeted like a rock, and his adrenaline soared. He really was going to be fired.

"You see, every five years we—Ethyl and I—have the chance to honor someone who exemplifies the type of person we want in this company. Someone who has worked hard, made a difference, and truly become a success. We have looked through hundreds of nominations, and this year we are choosing to honor you."

At first Troy's reaction was to think this was a big prank; he looked at his boss—*the* boss—and he knew it wasn't a joke. Then Troy was filled with bewilderment. "What?" Troy blurted without thinking. He wasn't going to be fired?

Eckhert looked nervous and started to backtrack.

"Well, yes. Unless you don't want to accept it." Troy could see that the award meant more to Eckhert than other awards, and the thought of someone turning it down was unexpected.

"No, no. I mean, yes! Yes, I'll accept it. It would be an honor." Troy started to laugh, the elation bubbling up inside like carbonation in a soda. "I thought you were going to fire me."

"What? Why on earth would you think something like that? You run one of the tightest offices in the whole company. That was enough for me to give you the award. But that's not what sold Ethyl." He leaned in as if telling a secret. "She's the hard one to please. What convinced her was the fact that you came from a poor background and never let that hold you back."

Troy thought of his mother and father and how proud they had been when he had graduated from college, when he had married Sarah, and when he had been hired by Eckhert Technology. He then thought of Sarah and how supportive she had been. He couldn't wait to tell her. His phone felt heavy against his leg. He was itching to text her right then.

"Thank you, sir. I'm not quite sure I know what to say. Tell Ethyl thank you too. I'm not sure that I deserve it."

"No need to say anything, son. I'll have my staff arrange things with your assistant. Do you like him, by the way? He seems a bit . . . nervous." Troy smiled at Eckhert's astute summary of Keith's demeanor this morning.

"Yes, Keith is great. He's been in the office since five this morning going over projects, thinking you were coming to discuss a problem."

Again, Eckhert laughed. "You have a high-strung bunch here, don't you? Well, it takes all types, and if it makes you as successful as you've been over the past few years, then keep them around."

Troy mumbled some kind of response and deliberated if Mr. Eckhert really understood the impact of showing up at any office other than his own. His entire presence made those under him squirm.

After the meeting, Troy walked dreamily back to his desk. He texted Sarah and told her that the meeting went well, making sure to convey he still had a job and that he would tell her all about it when he got home. Selfishly, he wanted to see her reaction as he told her. He also knew Sarah would want to know every detail, something he couldn't just text.

He turned to his computer and opened his email. Eckhert's staff had already given Keith the information for the award event, and he seemed relieved as well. It was to take place in Los Angeles at a gala. The email specified that the Eckherts were sponsoring the flights for himself, Sarah, and two other guests of their choice.

At first he wished that his parents were still alive—they would love to be there. Then he looked up and saw the plaque on the wall: "You're Better Than That." He knew exactly whom to invite.

12

Troy Walker

Troy strummed his fingers on the laminate table of the Diner as he waited for James to show up. James wasn't late, of course; Troy was early. For some reason he had the jitters about asking James to attend the award ceremony. He didn't want it to come across the wrong way. It was a tad bit awkward to tell someone you are being awarded without being pompous. Troy had discussed it with Sarah the night he found out, and she agreed that James and Molly were the right choice. After all, James had changed Troy's life and been his friend longer than anyone else.

The nice waitress who had seated him earlier came back a few times to make sure he didn't need anything. He didn't. He kept watching out the dirty windows for James.

Troy was still not sure how to ask James. He didn't want to sound arrogant about it. James truly was one of his heroes. Not only had he straightened him out in college, James continued to impress him. Not a man to cry easily, Troy had felt tears well up when he'd found out what James had done at his work to save jobs in his company. That was the type of man James was—humble and compassionate. Troy's award was nothing compared to the man James was.

Just then James came into the Diner. Troy jumped up to welcome him with a big hug. It was good to see James. No matter how long it had been, he and James were always comfortable with each other.

"How're you doing?" Troy asked, finally able to breathe now that James was actually there.

"I'm all right. Completely distracted with work, but doing all right otherwise." James's answer hinted of anxiety, Troy noted. He shrugged. James must just be busy.

"How are Molly and the kids doing?" James seemed to relax with that question, and the two of them swapped stories of family.

The rest of lunch went by in a blur. Troy never found a time to ask James. Every time he went to ask, the words sounded awkward in his head, and he ended up not bringing it up. Finally, as they were walking out of the Diner, Troy knew it was his last chance. He had to ask.

As they exited the building, Troy turned to his old friend.

"James, I want to invite you and Molly to join Sarah and me at an event." He shifted nervously as James watched him. "My work is giving me an award, and they offered to pay for two guests of honor to attend with us. Sarah and I want it to be you and Molly." There. It was out. Now he waited for his response.

James looked a bit dazed for a minute. "An award?" James looked down at his feet but quickly returned his gaze to Troy's face. "That's great. Really great, Troy. I'm happy for you."

Troy watched James and tried to decode his body clues. His words and his body language conflicted. James had accepted, but he seemed really distracted. Afterward, Troy worried all the way home if he had offended James in some way. He would have to call and give James the details later and check in. After all, you can't disappoint the hero that changed your life forever.

"Sarah?" Troy called out as he stepped into the front door of their home.

"Yes? I'm in here." He followed her voice into the kitchen and saw that she was stirring some kind of sauce on the stove. He walked over and gave her a kiss on the cheek.

"I talked with James today."

"Oh? And how did it go?"

Once again, Troy didn't know what to say. "Ah . . . he accepted, but he was . . ." *How to describe it?* "He was distracted. Almost like he was upset about it."

Sarah turned from her sauce and listened, concern appearing on her face. "James? Upset? Why would he be upset? I figured he would be happy. Maybe he was having a bad day at work."

Troy thought about it. Sarah was probably right. "He did say that he was busy today. Maybe that's it."

Sarah slapped him lovingly on the shoulder. "Since when did you become such a worrier about what other people think? Go get the kids. Dinner is almost ready."

Troy smiled. "What would I do without you?" He was glad Sarah saw things with a different perspective.

"You'd starve! Now go! My sauce is burning." She pushed him toward the door.

"So does that mean you'll call Molly tomorrow and set up the details too?" he called over his shoulder, laughing.

13

Selma Tobin

All things come to an end.

So this is it, Selma thought to herself as she picked up the fancy fountain pen to sign the divorce papers. A big life change, and she was here alone except for her lawyer and her husband—soon to be ex-husband—Karl's lawyer. He didn't even have the decency to be present. After five years of marriage, he had just quit.

The pen felt so heavy in her hand—both physically and emotionally. What had gone wrong? She had continually asked this question to herself over and over the last few months. The truth was, Selma discovered, there wasn't just *one* thing that went wrong. It was a collection of selfish actions, torn decisions, unsolved problems, and unattended needs that piled up over the years until one day it was all over.

Karl's lawyer made an impatient guttural sound for Selma to hurry. Selma guessed that divorce lawyers must become immune to emotions—all they see is the paycheck. *Don't they understand that these are people's lives they're signing away?* she thought as she straightened the papers and started to sign. The blue ink made the nightmare she had been living the last few months a final reality.

As Selma turned over the last page, a wave of trepidation restricted her breathing, and tears suddenly spilled down her cheeks. She was officially a single mom. She thought of her sons, Ian and Lucas. Ian was just over three years old, and Lucas was not yet one. How would they handle the change? How would she? Yes, Karl had been nearly absent over the recent months, but to have him completely gone from the home would leave a void. She put the pen to the page and signed her name one last time.

She stood suddenly. The room was claustrophobic. Both lawyers were staring at her with their blank, just-another-day-at-the-office faces. Her sadness transformed quickly into anger as she walked wordlessly past them. She needed a place to be alone. She was going to lose control of her emotions soon, and she didn't want it to be in front of these two insensitive paper custodians and their false concern. This was all too much.

Selma yanked open the glass door of the conference room they had been sitting in and headed down the hallway without looking back. Her vision was blurring as fast as her feet were walking. She found the elevators, but knowing the wait was too long, she dashed for the solid metal door with a staircase emblem painted on it. One dim yellow light lit each landing of the stairwell, and all she could see was gray cinder block and metal. The clicks of her heels echoed off the walls as she started down the first flight. Selma didn't even remember what floor the lawyer's office had been on. It didn't really matter. She was on her way out.

The heavy door of the stairwell shut with a thunderous

finality behind her. Closed. Just like her marriage. With that thought, another wave of tears arose.

Selma yelped—or cried—with the abrupt intensity of her emotions. They were no longer only her thoughts; her entire body was revolting. She stumbled and would have gone barreling down the stairs had she not caught herself on the cold metal railing. Slowly, she slid to the dirty stair halfway between floors, and the dam she had been trying to delay finally broke.

14

Selma Tobin

Selma had kept Karl's last name—Tobin—even though she knew that people would look at her as the desperate ex-wife who couldn't let go of what she'd had. That wasn't the situation, though. Selma actually had contemplated changing her name back to her maiden name, but eventually she decided against it for the boys. Their last name was Tobin, and she wanted to be a family as much as possible. The fabric of her family had been torn into two pieces. She was fighting to keep the edges that remained from fraying any more than they had to.

The boys had been through so many changes lately—if she could save them from a few more, no matter how small, it was worth it.

Selma had met Karl while he was in college and she was working as a manager of a small clothing shop near the school. He had come in one day looking for a tie to wear. His blond hair and green eyes had captured her that day.

She suggested that he buy a light-green tie to bring out the colors. He had laughed when she told him that, but rather than being offended, she had been exhilarated and unexpectedly attracted to his joy.

They had dated for over a year before they were married. A year later Ian was born. Both of them had been so happy to have a baby. Selma loved to watch Karl dote on Ian as a newborn, and she fell even more in love with the two men in her house during that time. Her naïve heart saw no worries, only a future full of happiness.

Karl started a job soon after graduation, and they were able to purchase their first home: the very home that Selma was still living in with the boys. Selma had wanted another baby, but when she would bring it up to Karl, he would divert the conversation. Selma should have seen the changes in Karl and their marriage. Selma pushed for another baby, and the more she pushed, the more his refusals became hostile.

They started to fight over little things—things that really didn't matter—but those fights indicated a problem that went deeper. Their relationship became strained. They spoke little when they were in the same room. Ian became a buffer for them—instead of focusing on each other and having a meaningful conversation, they invested all their attention on their son and never sorted out their problems. Instead the wounds were concealed and ripped brutally open again with each fight.

After months of Selma asking Karl for a baby, he had finally conceded. She had hoped the baby would bring back the feeling in their relationship that Ian had brought when he was born. Then they had a fight that Selma would never forget, a fight that was different from all the others because of its result.

Selma was several months pregnant, and they were fighting over towels. Towels. Who fought about towels?

"Karl! Why didn't you fold the towels? I asked you to fold the towels!" Selma yelled from the laundry room. She had had a long day, and this was the only thing she had asked him to do beyond watching Ian while she was out. "Karl!" she yelled again when he didn't respond to her first call. In response, she heard the volume of the game he was watching being turned up louder. The act infuriated her.

She stormed into the living room, ripped the remote out of his hand, and pushed the power button to kill the TV.

"What are you *doing,* Selma? I was watching that game!" Karl's yell was cold.

"You were not! You were ignoring me like you always do. I asked you why you didn't fold the towels like I asked. I asked you to do only one thing, and you couldn't stand up long enough to do it!" Selma felt herself lose control. She was shaking with rage.

"Why does it matter? We just use them anyway. I just saved a step. Why are you always nagging me?" Karl matched her pitch.

"Nagging? *Nagging*? That's what I do, huh? Nag?" The fury in Selma was rising to an explosive point.

"Yeah! Just like you are now! You're always yelling about something."

"I wouldn't have to *nag* you if you would just help around here! I'm pregnant. I don't feel well. I cook. I clean. I watch Ian. All I ask is for some help. It's like you don't even care!" Selma gestured wildly around the room.

Karl stood up, fuming with anger. Selma took an unsure step back. Karl's eyes were hard. She had never seen that before. Suddenly she was scared that he was going to strike her.

"Maybe I don't care!" he boomed.

"So you admit it!" Selma felt a surge of strength. He was admitting he was in the wrong.

"Yes, I don't care! I don't care to help. I don't care about the towels. I don't care what you do all day because I don't love you anymore!" Those words snuffed out the strength Selma thought she had. Surely he couldn't mean what he just said. Selma felt exposed and vulnerable as Karl's anger seemed to build.

"Arrgh!" Karl growled, grabbed the remote, and threw it; it shattered against the far wall. He exhaled and clenched his fists as he paced back and forth in the living room. Karl stopped in front of Selma, and she could see that his face was red, and the veins on his neck were straining under the hot adrenaline. "You don't get it, do you! I haven't loved you for the last year. I met someone at work, and I want to be with her now. I don't need you or your nagging anymore. And don't you *ever* use being pregnant as an excuse to argue with me. I never wanted that baby. You did! So you can keep the baby and your stupid towels. I'm done."

Selma had instinctively covered her stomach with both hands, as if to protect the baby from the harsh words. Karl scowled at her folded hands and stormed out of the house, slamming the door so hard the windows rattled. A favorite photograph of their wedding day fell over on the mantelpiece.

Vaguely, Selma realized that Ian was crying in his room. The noise must have woken him up. Hazily, she made her way to him. She cradled him in her arms, numbly whispering over and over, "It's all right. It's all right."

Lucas had been born a few days later, and Karl had called only to say that he had an appointment he couldn't miss. Selma had listened to the lie and heard the laugh of the woman in the background. Selma knew he had already moved on.

She never saw him face-to-face again.

Once, when Selma was a child, she had accidentally

knocked a crystal glass off a countertop. She remembered watching, shocked, as the glass had fallen in slow motion, hurdling to its shattered demise. She felt, in the days following Lucas's birth, that her life had become as fragile as that crystal glass. No matter how slow the fall appeared, she could not stop it—she could only watch it fall until the once beautiful piece of art broke into millions of shards.

Selma opened her eyes. The sheets were tangled around her body. She must have been thrashing again. She hated to dream about that fight and the roller-coaster experience of divorce over the last seven months. She lay there staring into the dark and felt the hollowness she had experienced yesterday on the steps of the law offices.

She vaguely recalled two kind women finding her in the stairwell and helping her get home. She hadn't even thanked them.

"Mom? Mom?" she heard Ian calling from the other room. She threw her covers back and walked down the hall to his door.

"What, honey? You're going to wake Lucas." She walked over to her little boy, who was sitting up in his bed. She sat down and wrapped her arms around his small frame. He was shaking. She hugged him tighter and kissed the top of his head. "What is it, buddy? What's the matter?"

"I don't want you to leave me." This was not an uncommon statement from Ian since Karl had left. Ian was worried that everyone else in his life would abandon him too.

New tears sprung into Selma's eyes, and she buried her face in Ian's hair. "I won't leave you. I love you so much. I'll never leave you. We are a family."

Selma was, in part, relieved that someone still loved and needed her, and sad in another that a three-year-old had to worry about life instead of just enjoying it.

Ian pushed back and looked Selma in the eye. She could see his earnest features even in the dim glow of his night-light. "And Lucas? He'll stay with us too? He's part of our family?" His questions were full of concern for his younger brother.

Selma smiled and pulled Ian in for another hug. "Yes, Lucas too. The three of us are a family. Do you want to come sleep with me tonight? We'll go get Lucas, and it will be like having a sleepover."

Selma lay wide awake long after Ian and Lucas had fallen asleep again, their little bodies snuggled up to her on either side. She again thought of the heartache it had caused her to see Karl leave. Somehow she had missed the fact that Ian and Lucas had lost him too. She was all they had.

Selma knew that while Karl had chosen to end their marriage and leave their lives, he was not the only one to blame. She was part of the relationship, and they had both made mistakes that caused them to grow apart. His infidelity had left her feeling exposed, insecure, and empty; however, she didn't have a choice—she had to move on. These two little boys sleeping next to her needed to feel safe. She was the only person to provide that safety for them.

Selma had come to the United States as an exchange student several years earlier on a scholarship program. Her parents were farmers and lived a hard life. A few years after being here she received a message from her aunt: Selma's parents had died in a fire that had burned down their small cottage during the night.

Selma had never been close to Karl's parents. They didn't approve of Karl marrying a "foreigner." They hadn't even come to the marriage, telling Karl that all Selma wanted was a green card. She was completely alone.

Selma knew it was going to be rough. Single parents never chose to be single parents. Life's journey had altered her course and landed the three of them in a situation they hadn't asked for. But it was up to them to make the best of it.

Holding the boys a little closer on each side, Selma vowed that she would better herself—for her boys.

15

Selma Tobin

Selma had been a single mother now for a little more than seven years.

Ian was now ten years old, and Lucas had just turned eight. Their lives over the last few years had developed a smooth rhythm.

Lucas had adapted the easiest. He had never known anything different than the family they had now, so he never questioned it.

Ian, for the most part, was the same, although he still remembered his father. Most of his memories were happy ones, though. Selma had made a point to not dampen those memories.

She tried to never speak ill of Karl in front of the boys. Karl had made that easy to do by completely staying out of their lives except for a few phone calls to Selma about some new excuse for not paying child support or some other court problem.

Karl and the "woman from work" hadn't lasted long and was the springboard into a life of chaos and trouble for Karl. He hadn't been able to hold a steady job and lived between new girlfriends' homes. Selma often thought that in many ways, their divorce was Karl's greatest present to her.

Selma planned to tell the boys about their father when they were ready. She figured that whenever they started to ask about Karl, she would tell them. So far they seemed content with the life she had tried to give them. And she was content to keep it that way, at least for now.

Lost in her thoughts, Selma drove to the school to pick the boys up, something she was happy to do each day. Her boss at work allowed a flexible schedule so she could come in early and leave early.

She couldn't explain, even to herself, the internal need to be there for the boys each day as they came out of the school toward the car. She used to tell herself that it gave the boys something constant in their chaotic life. However, she had since realized that a more selfish motive was behind the act as well. The moment she saw those two smiling faces, no matter how rough the day had been, her heart fluttered with gratitude. Those rare moments were a respite from her otherwise cloudy world.

Today was no different.

She parked the car in her usual place next to all the other parents. As she waited, Selma's attention was captured by one of the other waiting mothers. She was talking on her cell phone, waving her hands frantically as if the person on the other end could see her. Selma almost laughed as she watched the woman's perfectly coiffed hair jerk back and forth with each gesture. She wondered who the mother could be talking to—hopefully not her husband. Ever since her divorce, Selma had hoped that no other woman would have to experience what she did with Karl.

"Hello! It's Ms. Tobin, right?" Selma turned and saw a woman with dark hair formed into a large halo-like bump. Selma thought about her own hair pulled back into a bun and wondered how these women had the time and patience to get their hair like that.

"Sorry to disturb you. I'm Livina Agosti. My daughter Rinna is in Ian's class. I've seen you at other school functions and wanted to say hello."

Selma reached out her hand. "Nice to meet you, Ms. Agosti."

"Oh, honey, you can just call me Livina."

"It is nice to meet you, Livina," Selma said with a smile.

"Rinna tells me that we don't live too far from your house. We should have lunch sometime."

"That would be nice. Thank you, Livina."

The school bell rang, and Selma looked toward the door. A flood of children in an array of color and voices fanned out of the doors. She watched for her boys. Then there they were.

Ian was walking in long strides. Selma noted how much he was changing as a ten-year-old. His legs were longer, and his mannerisms, despite the limited amount of time he had spent with Karl, were so much like his father. Lucas followed in his short bouncy steps, trying to keep up with his older brother.

Selma smiled to see that Lucas was talking nonstop, looking up intently at his brother's face as he retold some story. She hoped the boys never grew apart. Lucas admired Ian so much.

"Hey, how are my two favorite men?" Selma greeted them as they slid into the car—Ian in the front next to her and Lucas in the back.

"Hi, Mom!" Lucas's reply was chipper. Selma adjusted her rearview mirror as she exited the school lot so she could see Lucas's face. He would always slide to the center of the backseat so he could lean forward and talk with them as they drove.

Selma liked to adjust the mirror to see the joyful expressions on his face as he experienced the world—his innocent world. Again Selma dreaded the day when she could no longer protect them.

She looked over to her older son, who was more quiet than usual. "How are you, handsome?" Selma smiled and watched him out of the corner of her eye.

"All right," Ian answered indifferently and turned his head to look out the window. Alarm bells sounded in Selma's ears. Something was wrong. She paused for a moment, wondering if she should push, but before she could say anything more, Lucas piped up from the back.

"Mom! Do you want to hear about science class today? I already told Ian, but he'll be okay to hear it again."

"Yes, tell me about it." Selma forced a cheerful voice to match Lucas's, though she continued to eye Ian as she drove.

"Today Mrs. Brase let us make a volcano! It was so awesome! It had fire and everything. Did you know that a volcano is caused by heat from lots of tiny chemical reactions? When all the pressure builds up under the rocks it explodes—kerplooosh!"

Selma looked in the mirror to see sheer glee on Lucas's face as he added sound effects to his story. His hands went up to the ceiling of the car and then out to mimic the explosion of the volcano. Selma couldn't help but laugh. Her little guy was always full of happiness.

"Well, then it's a good thing you didn't burn the school down," Selma said, still laughing.

Lucas turned serious, and his face knit with concern over his mother's worry. "It's all right, Mom. Mrs. Brase made sure we were all safe. And it wasn't real fire."

Selma's heart began to warm again. "Well, I'll have to tell Mrs. Brase thanks for keeping my little man safe, won't I?"

"I already told her for you!"

"You did? What did you say?" This conversation was becoming more and more interesting.

"I told her thanks for keeping me safe because you need someone to give you a hug at night, and I am your best hugger!"

"Yes, you are. I need hugs from you and Ian both." Selma tried to bring Ian back into the conversation, but he was still staring blankly out his window.

They arrived at home with Lucas filling them in on the rest of his day. Science class was indeed the highlight, and they heard every detail, including how, when the fake volcano had exploded, Jane had screamed so loud that the principal ran to see what was wrong. Lucas was laughing so hard as he told the story that he couldn't finish. His laughter was contagious, and Selma joined in.

"Lucas, that's a fun story, but I hope you didn't make Jane feel bad by laughing at her in front of everyone else."

"Oh, no. She was all right. Once she realized the lava wasn't really lava, and it didn't burn her, she laughed too."

Selma parked at the house, and both boys jumped out. Selma followed them in and was saddened to see that Ian went straight to his room and shut the door. She would have to talk with him before the night was over.

She found Lucas in the kitchen digging through the pantry for something to eat. Selma was beginning to realize that boys really were always hungry—and hers weren't even teenagers yet. "Hey, buddy, I'm going to make dinner. Don't ruin your appetite."

"What're you fixing?" Lucas looked up briefly from the pantry.

"I was thinking tacos. Is there something else you want?"

"Yay! Tacos are our favorite!"

Selma set to work fixing dinner, but her thoughts kept drifting to her oldest son shut in his bedroom. Although she asked Lucas about the tacos, Selma wanted to make them for Ian. He loved tacos, which is why Lucas did too. He loved anything Ian liked. She wanted to do something that would cheer Ian up. Or at least get him out of his room.

"Lucas, thank you for your help. Do you want to get your brother for dinner?" Lucas obediently went down the hall, and Selma could hear the muffled voices of her sons as she put the last few items for dinner on the table.

The boys sat down, and once again Selma fought the urge to barrage Ian with questions. Instead, she focused on having a nice meal. Dinnertime was a special time for her. It was another part of their lives she had tried to keep steady. They may not have been a traditional family in the mother-father-children sense, but she wanted to show the boys that they were a family, and time together was important. Having dinner together, no matter how meager or fast, was one of the ways Selma felt she was holding her fragile life together.

Ian at least participated in the conversation throughout dinner. He had minimal input, but it was enough that Lucas didn't notice. As dinner ended, Selma asked them, "Do you have homework? I can do the dishes so you can finish it. We need to get to bed on time so we aren't late in the morning."

Both boys rushed off to do their homework, most likely happy to not have to help with the dishes. As she mindlessly cleaned the kitchen, Selma thought of countless different situations that could explain why Ian would be having a hard time. The phone rang, and, still lost in thought, Selma answered it without checking the caller ID.

"Hello?" Even to Selma, her cheerful voice sounded fake.

"We need to talk."

Selma just about dropped the phone and the plate she

was drying. It was Karl. Of course there was no "hello," no "how are the boys?" Internally she sighed. Karl was still selfish. Some things just never change.

"Karl?" Selma asked, even though she knew full well who it was. She wondered what inane problem he wanted to waste her time with this time.

"Selma, I'm selling the house." His words were hard, and Selma felt her breath rush out of her in disbelief.

"What? Karl, what are you saying?" Sudden tears pricked at her eyes.

"You heard me. I'm selling the house."

"You can't do that!"

"The house is still technically in my name, so I can do with it as I please."

"But where will we live?" Selma's voice became shrill.

"I don't care where you live; I just want the money." Selma's mind went racing through her options. Should she plead with Karl to not do this? Should she argue with him? She then realized that she and Karl had never had a sensible conversation. She might as well not start.

"Good-bye, Karl." With shaking hands, Selma hung up the phone. Wiping away the tears that were falling freely now, she walked over to the drawer across the kitchen where she kept her address book and thumbed through until she found the number for her lawyer.

A company answering machine picked up, announcing that the law offices were closed in a voice that, to Selma, sounded way too perky. After she heard the tone chime, Selma left a message about the situation and asked for someone to call back as soon as they could.

Selma didn't think the night could get worse. But it did.

16

Selma Tobin

"*Who was that?*" Selma jumped at the sound of the voice. She realized she was still sitting in the kitchen with the phone in her hands. She quickly wiped her tears, hung up the phone, and looked up to see Ian watching her. She wondered how long he had been there, and if he had overheard the call.

"Nobody," Selma said, forcing a smile. She didn't want to bring the boys into the mess their father had created for them—yet. She wanted to wait until she knew what was happening before she worried them.

"It was Dad, wasn't it?" It was more of a statement of disdain than a question.

Selma didn't know how to answer. She wouldn't lie to him, but she couldn't bring herself to talk about it either—at least, not without breaking down and crying.

Selma noticed something else funny about Ian's question—she was surprised to hear Ian mention Karl. They never, ever talked about him.

Ian knew Selma's silence was confirmation. Selma knew that Ian knew it too.

"Why did you kick him out?" Ian's question burned.

"What?" Selma was at a loss for words. She could feel Ian's anger boiling, and she wasn't sure she understood what he had just said.

"Why did you kick dad out of our lives? Why can't we be just a normal family?"

"I . . . I . . ." Selma stumbled over her answer. "Ian, I didn't kick your father out of our lives. He chose to leave."

"All the other kids at school have both parents! Why is it that we only have *you*?" His words were a hard slap to Selma's face. Hurt, Selma paused to think this through before she commented. She knew Ian loved her and was just angry. Maybe this was what had been bothering him earlier.

Choosing to ignore that he just insinuated she was not good enough for him, Selma asked, "What do you mean, Ian?"

"I mean that I'm sick of having to be different!" Ian was shaking with anger now. Tears ran down his face. Selma knew that like Lucas's volcano, Ian must have been holding in some emotions, and they were finally exploding. She suppressed the impulse to stand up and hug him as she used to when he was younger. "Did Lucas tell you about next week?" Ian asked.

That question threw Selma off. "No. What about next week?"

"Did he tell you that they are having a father-and-son day at school? He wants me to be his 'dad' for the day. I'm not his dad!" Ian was getting louder and louder. "Why do I have to be his dad? Why can't we have a real dad?"

Selma's whole world became myopic. All that mattered was the three of them: Ian, Lucas, and herself. She pushed aside all worries about Ian's reaction and stood up to fold him into her arms. He stood stiffly for a few minutes and cried, but eventually he too wrapped his arms around her.

All Selma could say was, "I'm sorry, Ian. I don't know why this happens. But I do know that I love you, and I love your brother. You are his hero, and you are one of my heroes too." She buried her face in his hair and held him until his tears stopped. "I'm sorry that your dad leaving us puts you in positions that you don't want to be in. I wish I could fix it, but I can't. I'm glad you are willing to do some of this. You're a good person, Ian. I love you."

Later that night, after Selma made sure both boys were in bed, she went to her own room, lay on her bed in the darkness, and stared at the ceiling. The boys needed to have a father figure in their lives. That wouldn't be Karl, for sure. He obviously had no interest in the boys, and she didn't want his type of example around them anyway.

In that moment Selma was thankful that Karl had left. It was emancipating. For years she had mourned his choice to leave them, but after tonight she realized that no matter how hard life was as a single mother, the boys would not be raised to believe that men should act as Karl did.

The problem was that her boys needed an example to follow, a man who would show them how to be men. But where would she find a man like that? Selma rolled over and saw how late it was. Knowing she had an early morning tomorrow, she knew she needed to force herself to sleep. She thought again of Karl's phone call. Tomorrow was bound to be a long day.

17

Selma Tobin

M*orning arrived faster* than Selma would have liked. She got out of bed feeling empty, emotionally and physically. She shuffled down the hallway to the boys' bedroom and made sure they both were awake before she headed to the kitchen. More often than not, both of them would fall asleep again after she had woken them up.

She cracked some eggs into a bowl and beat them for scrambled eggs. Selma learned on her tight budget that eggs were a solid food that would fill her growing boys' stomachs and give them energy for the day. As she cooked, she listened to the sounds of preparation coming from the other end of the house, and her mind slipped back into the nightmare of last night.

The phone rang, slicing through the silence. Panic rose in her throat. What if it was Karl again? Selma walked over and picked up the phone. The orange LCD screen read, "James and Molly Smith." Such a rush of relief coursed over Selma that she almost cried. Only then did she realize how panicked she had been.

"Good morning," Selma found herself saying into the receiver, walking back to the eggs that were still crackling on the stove.

"Selma, sorry to call you so early, but I wanted to catch you before I went to work." Selma was happy to hear a twinge of grogginess in Molly's friendly voice. Even mothers who had a husband to help had hard mornings it seemed. Selma didn't know Molly well, but her son Jaden was a friend of Ian's. They had met briefly several times at mutual activities. Molly was always kind to Selma.

"No, I'm just cooking breakfast." Selma played down the fact that she was still in her pajamas and looked like she just survived an earthquake.

"I'm calling to see if you would be interested in having your boys play baseball this year. James coaches Jaden's team, and they are a few players short. The whole league needs to add a couple players so they can actually have full teams. When James told us about it last night at dinner, Jaden and I thought Ian and Lucas would be wonderful additions to the team."

"Ahh . . ." Selma was at a loss for words. She had never considered having the boys play sports. She didn't have the money for extracurricular activities.

Molly heard the hesitation and rushed to explain. "It's all right if you don't want them to. I just wanted to give you an opportunity."

"No, it's okay, Molly. I'm glad you called. It's just that I have never asked the boys if they would like to play sports competitively. I'll need to ask them and get back to you. When do you need to know?"

"Well . . ." It was Molly's turn to hesitate. "The teams are picking their players tomorrow. I'm so sorry I didn't call sooner. I know it is kind of a rush decision. Again, it's okay if it doesn't work out."

"Molly, really, it's all right. Let me talk to the boys this morning, and I'll get back to you."

Selma hung up the phone and thought about the situation. Her first thought was money. After last night, she realized that soon she might not even have a house. Playing baseball seemed so inconsequential to the prospect of being homeless.

But then she remembered her thoughts about needing good men to be examples to her sons. Jaden was a good kid, and Ian liked him well enough. James was always good to the boys when he saw them. Maybe this was an answer. Maybe they would have something positive to focus on if Karl succeeded in throwing their world into chaos again.

As the boys sat down to eat, Selma found herself hoping they would find playing baseball a good idea too. "Jaden's mom, Molly, called me this morning." Both boys looked up at her. "She asked if you two would be interested in playing on Jaden's baseball team this year. Jaden's dad is the coach, and they need a few more players."

Ian's eyes sparked immediately, and Selma knew she had made the right decision. It was worth everything she would have to sacrifice to pay for it—and after last night's talk, it was enchanting to see him happy.

"Really?" Ian said. "We can do that? I told Jaden that we probably wouldn't be able to."

Selma wanted to let them know that this wasn't going to be easy, but they could do it. "Well, we may have to sacrifice a little so we can come up with the extra money, but if you two are willing to help out, we can do it."

Lucas exclaimed, "Even me? I can play too?" He said the words to Selma, but he was looking at Ian for assurance that his brother approved of him playing. Selma waited to see what Ian would do. She silently willed him to say the right thing. After last night she didn't know what to expect.

Finally Ian smirked and said, "Of course you can play

too. You're eight, aren't you? Jaden said that eight-year-olds can be on the team too." Selma's worries relieved just a bit.

After she dropped the boys off at school, Selma called and told Molly that the boys would love to play and got all the details they would need. As they were talking, Selma's phone beeped with call waiting. She looked quickly and saw that it was the lawyer's office. "Molly, I have another call I need to take. Thank you so much for thinking of my boys today. It made a huge difference."

"Jaden will be excited too."

Selma quickly hung up and took a deep breath before answering the lawyer's waiting call. "Hello?"

"Selma, sorry that I didn't get back to you quicker," her lawyer said. "I wanted to follow up on a few things before I called you. I am so sorry that you are going through this. It must have been a rough night."

Selma rolled her eyes. Her lawyer was good to her and tried to be compassionate; however, her experience with the divorce had taught her that what all lawyers really wanted was your money. "Thank you for calling me back." She remained formal. Although she knew that his reasons to help were unclear, she did need his help after all.

"I have some good news for you."

Selma almost burst out laughing when she heard that. She wasn't prepared to have a conversation that contained the words "good news."

"This is why I took so long to call you. I was waiting to hear back from Judge Gurchel." Judge Gurchel was the judge who oversaw the divorce and the child custody.

Selma waited patiently for the news. Her lawyer continued, "I was in shock about Karl's phone call, just as you were, I'm sure. I went back and looked into the records and saw that the house is indeed in Karl's name. Because of that he does technically have the right to sell the house."

I thought this was supposed to be good, Selma thought.

"I say technically because I also looked back at the court ruling, and it specifically states that you will remain living there. And as I understand you have been making the payments, am I correct?"

Selma felt a glimmer of hope. "Yes," she answered cautiously. "I've been making the payments since the day Karl walked out." Selma didn't even try to withhold the seething venom she felt.

"Good, and I also know that Karl has not been paying the child support that he owes you either, correct?"

"No, he hasn't," Selma responded, frustrated. The only thing that kept her from yelling, "Get to the point!" was the fact that her lawyer was the only object between her and homelessness.

"Great!"

That did it; she had to say something. "Not to be rude, but I thought you were going to give me good news. How is my ex-husband not paying years of child support great?" Tears stung her eyes as she said this. If there was ever time she sounded desperate, it was right now.

"Oh, I'm sorry, Selma. I get caught up in the details sometimes. I didn't mean to drag this on. To make this short, Karl cannot sell the house because he hasn't been paying child support for Ian and Lucas over the last seven years. I added it up, and the price in back payments is more than enough to have the house declared yours. All I needed was Judge Gurchel's approval. There are no promises until we bring it before the court officially in a few days, but Judge Gurchel was supportive. Until then, I went ahead and reinstated the restraining order that states Karl cannot come near you or your sons until something is decided."

The room around Selma melted into a blur as she started crying again, this time with joy. Maybe she would have to rethink her stereotype of lawyers.

18

Selma Tobin

"*Connie, thank you* for taking that last spreadsheet. I owe you one," Selma called over her shoulder as she went out of the office door. The boys had a game today, and she needed to get home to help them get ready.

Having the boys play baseball was one of the best decisions she had made as a mother. Of course it had been a gamble—at the time she'd had no idea how she could afford it—but with the court order stating that Karl had to pay child support and the house was hers, she had money to care for her sons.

Over the past few weeks all Selma heard from both of them was "baseball this" or "James that." Just as Selma had hoped, James's positive attitude had rubbed off on the boys. She had never liked sports before. She'd detested them even when Karl tried to get her to like them. In her mind, sports were a waste of time. She hated to watch Karl get sucked into zombie zone while watching some sports channel. But

James and the boys were slowly convincing her that she was a fan of baseball.

Selma arrived home to frantic shouts from Lucas's room. "Where are my socks?"

Ian answered his younger brother with impatience. "Did you look under your bed? You have to hurry! We can't be late!"

Selma rounded the corner and saw them both in various stages of uniform. "Yes, if you both don't hurry, you'll be late. I'll get your socks. I washed them last night for you. They are sitting on the dryer. I left a note on the fridge for you that said that." She retrieved the socks and came back in to help Lucas finish getting ready.

"Mom?" Lucas asked as he pulled on his clean socks.

"Yeah?"

"What if I'm not as good as the other kids?"

"What do you mean, Lucas?"

"Coach has to help me more than the other kids because I'm small and not very good. What if I strike out again? Will they hate me?"

Selma knelt down next to her son, who was sitting on his bed. "No. No, Lucas. Coach James helps you because he wants you to get better."

"But all the other kids are so big. I'm so small."

"Lucas, you're two years younger than them. When you're ten you will be just as tall as they are. You'll do fine. Coach James, Ian, and I will be there cheering you on. Just like we always do." She reached up and cupped her hand around his face.

"Thanks, Mom."

"Come on, let's go before your brother gets frantic," Selma said, and Lucas laughed as they headed out the door.

Selma found a place in the bleachers so she could see the entire field and the Near World team dugout. The game was a close one. James did well with the boys. They didn't win often, but watching James yell and encourage each of them showed her that he really cared.

It was the last inning of the game, and two Near World players were on base. Selma could feel herself getting nervous for them. She sat on her hands in an attempt to calm her nerves. It only made it worse. She looked up to see who was up to bat next, and her heart dropped to see Lucas step out.

Despite her pep talk in the bedroom earlier, she noted how small he looked out on the field—her baby, her bundle of cheer drowning in a Near World jersey. He stepped out to do a few practice swings, mimicking his brother. Lucas looked up to her in the stands as he always did. Selma put a smile on her face, as big as she could, and waved in encouragement. Her heart was doing gymnastics. "Please let him succeed. Please let him hit," she murmured. The suspense in the crowd was dense. The entire game rested on Lucas's performance.

Selma couldn't handle the thought that Lucas would fail. Her son was facing the very fears he had been worried about. Here he was at the center of the game. The entire outcome weighed on his shoulders. Her motherly instincts kicked in, and she wanted to protect him from the pain of failure. She knew she couldn't, though. All she could do was hope.

She watched as her brave little guy walked up to the plate. The pitcher wound up and threw a hard ball. Lucas swung, but he was far too late. Selma winced in pain as she saw it happen.

"It's all right, Lucas!" she called to him. "It's all right. Keep your eye on the ball! Get the next one." After a few games she had learned the proper baseball lingo so she wouldn't embarrass her boys by yelling what she truly wanted to—phrases like "Mommy loves you!"—which is exactly what she meant when she yelled, "You have this, Lucas!"

The pitcher, looming much taller from the mound, threw a second pitch. "Strike two!" the umpire yelled. Selma saw Lucas's shoulders drop in discouragement, and her heart dropped too. *Come on! Let him hit the ball!* she prayed.

"You can do it, Lucas!" she yelled loudly and heard all of the other fans cheering him on too. Lucas stood back and swung the bat a few times and bravely stepped up to the plate once again. The pitcher threw, and Selma fought the itch to close her eyes. The suspense was chilling. Lucas swung, and the metal bat pinged as Lucas connected with the ball. Selma and all the other Near World fans leapt to their feet, screaming.

"Go! Go! Go!"

Selma was vaguely aware of the entire crowd cheering along with her as the play unfolded before them. The ball bounced softly to the second baseman. Selma willed Lucas to run faster. She watched in agony as he neared first base. The ball arrived just before he did, and the umpire yelled, "Out!" Half the crowd moaned, and the other half, fans for the other team, broke out in applause.

Selma had eyes for only one little boy who struggled to walk back to the dugout. His pain was her pain. *Devastation* was the only word Selma could use to describe it.

She wanted to run out and hug him. She made her way down the bleachers through all of the people leaving and looked up to see James walking briskly across the field toward Lucas. Selma tensed—he was angry; she knew it. She started to walk faster. She was not going to let some man bully her son over a stupid game.

Selma reached the chain-link fence of the field at the same time James met Lucas. Selma was close enough to see the tears streaming down Lucas's dusty face. To Selma's surprise, James didn't yell at Lucas or even talk to him. James dropped to his knees, put his hand under Lucas's chin, and wiped away a tear with his thumb. Selma saw Lucas say something to James, but she didn't hear what it was.

Selma saw James's expression change. His chin began to quiver, and in one swoop he pulled Lucas into his embrace. Selma saw tears coming down James's face too just before she too had tears blur everything but the outline of the two people along the first baseline.

Selma was so thankful in that moment for Molly's call several weeks earlier. That invitation to play baseball could very well shape the lives of her two growing sons. Yes, James was the example Selma wanted her sons to learn from—a man who made a positive difference in people's lives.

19

Halbert Germaine

"*Mornin', Hal!" Rita* called from her front porch as Hal carried a few chairs out of the house.

"Mornin', Rita! How yeh doin'?"

"Mighty fine. We've got a big day ahead celebratin'," Rita called back. Hal and his wife, Frances, had lived on the narrow Dunbar Street for thirty-five years. Rita, their neighbor, prided herself on living there longer.

She had moved there two years earlier than them when the brown, square row houses were new. Rita's children had grown up with Hal and Frances's five children. This neighborhood was family. They celebrated together, they cried together, and they stayed in each other's business. Frances often joked there were no secrets on Dunbar.

The narrow street boasted eighteen row houses, nine on each side. The brown brick homes with white trim had seen many children playing games on summer nights. Families had come and gone, and children had run from home to home, playing one game or another. Dunbar Street was a refuge for all of them.

Hal set the two chairs he was carrying next to the wooden picket fence that separated their yard from Rita's and the slow traffic along the street. Hal and his oldest son, Jackson, had painted it last week so it would be ready for today.

Rita was right; today was a day of celebration. Today, Rhonda, Hal's second child, turned twenty-four and graduated from college.

Hal loved all his children for different reasons, but Rhonda was his princess. She was born a year after Jackson and had stolen his heart. He was proud of her.

Frances had told all their children they would get an education. Neither Hal nor Frances had had the opportunity to attend college after high school. Because of it, life was hard. They weren't going to let their children have that experience. Education was the key to the door of opportunities.

Frances and Hal had worked hard to make that dream a reality. Frances washed and ironed clothes for other people for hours on end. The money she made was used to make the home comfortable. Every penny Hal made went toward their home and the children's education.

Jackson finished a few years ago and was working on his law degree in the city. Rhonda was graduating with a degree in psychology. Rita always joked that Rhonda became a "shrink" after living on Dunbar for twenty years. Hal deliberated who was more proud about today: Rhonda, him, or Frances.

As if she had heard his thoughts, Rita called out, "I'm mighty proud of that girl." Hal chuckled to himself. Maybe Rita was the most proud today.

"Daddy, Mamma wants you in the kitchen," Lydia, their baby, said as she went up the stairs to her bedroom.

Lydia was seventeen and the last of their children to be in high school. Carson and Rafael, twenty-one and nineteen, were both enrolled in a community college, getting their general education classes finished.

Frances and Hal had taken out a second mortgage on their home to pay for their education. It was something Frances had struggled with at first. She was afraid of losing the house and everything they had worked for. Hal had finally convinced her that the second mortgage would help the children get their education, and with his steady job, they would be all right. She finally consented.

"Okay, baby, I'll go see what she wants," Hal said as he entered the house.

Lydia laughed as she climbed the staircase. "Good luck! You know how Mamma gets on days like this. She wants everything to be *perfect*."

Hal smiled to himself. Lydia was right. Frances was a perfectionist when it came to two things: her house and her children. And he had learned long ago not to stand in her way on those two platforms. When Frances was in her "work mode," it was in your best interest to ask where you can help and perform the action assigned to you as quickly and flawlessly as possible.

Hal walked into the chaotic kitchen. Frances was the conductor of an orchestra of hands. Everyone who crossed the threshold of the kitchen was given a job, even if they didn't ask for one. "Mamma, Lydia said you needed me."

Frances looked up from some dough she was kneading on the center island. Hal laughed a throaty laugh as he saw his beautiful wife, usually impeccable in her appearance, covered in flour. He loved that woman; he had for years.

"What?" she asked but then carried on before he could answer. "Did you get the chairs out?" Again she rushed on before he could answer. "I need you to fill the cooler out on the back steps with ice and water for the soda."

Hal smiled again and headed out the back door to do her bidding. Frances had already gone back to her bread knowing full well he would do as she asked. They worked like that, she and he. Years of struggle, trial, and error had taught them to respect one another. They were not perfect—nobody is—but they knew one another's strengths and weaknesses and worked hard to complement each other. It wasn't easy, but when has anything worth it been easy? And to Hal, Frances was worth it.

The night was perfect. Laughter and stories abounded as neighbors came and filled long buffet tables with food of all kinds. They celebrated long into the night. Carson and Rafael surprised all the kids with some fireworks they had stored from the Fourth of July.

Hal found himself sitting on the porch on the double swing with Frances. He reached over for her small, warm hands. He loved her more now than he could ever imagine.

She looked up from the melee of squeals and laughter coming from the street as their sons lit sparklers for the children, and squeezed his hand lovingly. "We're going to be all right, aren't we, Hal?"

"Yes, we are. Yes, we are." It felt good to finally say that with conviction. Over the years neither Hal nor Frances thought they were going to make it, but their hard work was paying off. Their children were growing to be strong men and women. Hal had plenty to be thankful for.

20

Halbert Germaine

H*al loved the* morning. The streets of the city in front of Near World were calm and serene during this time. In a few short hours, these same streets would be full of loud noises—honking cars, yelling pedestrians, and plenty of other sounds that would fill the air. For twenty-eight years Hal had worked there on the same street as a doorman for the Near World building. The stories he could tell about the people on these streets were shocking. He had come to know that the unexpected is normal.

Hal could retire in two years if he wanted to, but he knew he couldn't do that with the new mortgage on the house and three more children to put through school. Today though, management informed him that a new guy, Kole, was going to be training with him. He knew his bosses were preparing for someone to take his place when he finally retired.

Being a doorman was an interesting career. You know

everyone, but no one. Everyone knows either your name or your face, but never both. Sometimes they know neither. Hal could tell you the names and ages of all the people that worked in the Near World building. He could point out their family members and those who had less respectable "friendships" with people not part of their families.

To Hal, these people were his life. To these people, Hal was invisible.

"I hope the new boy is cut out for this," Hal mumbled to himself as he shined the ornate brass handles on the doors. The only reason Hal stayed here was for his family. To be fair, Hal knew that not everyone ignored him. Some of them genuinely seemed to know him.

"Hey! Are you Hal?" Hal turned quickly—he hadn't even heard the kid walk up. That was unusual for a seasoned doorman; Hal was usually aware of someone approaching the building long before they arrived. Hal was staring at a skinny red-haired boy no older than his son Carson. Had he not been wearing a maroon suit identical to Hal's, Hal would have kindly asked him to keep walking as he did with all the other tourists who asked for a toilet or a Tylenol.

"That's me. You must be Kole."

The boy straightened up with pride to hear his name. "Yes, that's me."

"Well, boy, the first thing you need to learn about the job is everyone that walks through these doors is your boss. You address them as 'sir' or 'ma'am.' You can start by practicing with me." Hal threw him some gloves for his hands. "Put these on. You'll need them to protect those skinny white fingers of yours."

Kole caught the gloves and looked up at Hal with fear. Hal started to laugh—the mirth rolled all the way from his toes until it filled him with warmth. "Look at you, kid; you look scared to death!"

Kole had finally realized that Hal was joking with him and started to laugh too.

"You need to lighten up! The people going in these doors are full of worries and stress. Your job is to bring a bit of brightness to their day." Hal paused for emphasis. "But never refer to them by anything but 'sir' or 'ma'am,' even if they tell you not to."

"Okay. I can do that," Kole said, flexing his hands in his new gloves.

"Eh . . . you're forgetting your first rule already?"

Kole stuttered, embarrassed. "Oh! Sorry. I mean, okay, sir, I can do that."

Hal smiled. "Good job. Now here's your first guest. This is Miss Susan Priar." Hal pointed up the road to the tall thin woman walking elegantly up the road in a bright pink skirt.

Kole lowered his voice and said, "Miss? But she's *old*."

Hal elbowed Kole quickly and said, "Keep your thoughts to yourself, boy—or at least until you get home to your wife . . . whenever you get one. Until then, smile and bring some happiness to your clients. Do you think pointing out Miss Priar's age is going to make her feel better about the day? Here, I'll show you how it's done. Watch closely because the next one is yours."

Hal walked out a few steps to greet Miss Priar as she arrived. "Good mornin', Miss Priar. How was your weekend?" He reached out to take Miss Priar's hand.

"Well, well. Thank you. Have you seen Mr. Barnes come in yet?" Typically, she was only worried about covering niceties before asking about her personal agenda.

"No, we haven't seen him yet," Hal answered as he walked her to the door and opened it for her.

"Oh, good. I have a report to finish before he gets here." And with that, Miss Priar wisped through the door, leaving only the scent of her flowery perfume to linger.

Hal turned to Kole, who was watching from the corner of the entry. "You see, boy, to them you're here to make their lives easier. To open the door, answer questions, and smile. Got that?"

"Yes . . . Yes, sir." Kole said, this time with a smile as wide as Hal's own.

For the next few hours, Hal introduced Kole to the Near World staff as they came in for work. Much to Hal's delight, Kole seemed like a natural. He remembered details that Hal told him as people walked up, like the fact that Mrs. Finch didn't like the door being opened for her; she preferred to do it herself. Or that Mr. Underson expected you to fold his umbrella for him if he was using one. And finally, what make and model Mr. Barnes's car was so that he never, ever missed a chance to open Mr. Barnes's door when he arrived.

Hal looked up and saw a man walking from the garage. He knew by his gait that it was Mr. Smith. "Kole," Hal said, nodding to the man approaching, "that there is Mr. Smith. He's the accountant for the company. He's the one that writes our paychecks. It would be to your best interest to know him."

James arrived and said cheerfully, "Good morning, Hal. Who's your new partner?" This was the other reason that Hal pointed Mr. Smith out to Kole—Mr. Smith always remembered Hal's name and would look him in the eye as he asked how his day was. That was uncommon. It was even more uncommon that Mr. Smith would stop for a few seconds and wait for Hal's response. Hal knew this man was busy running all the business of Near World, but he made Hal feel like he had all the time in the world to stop and chat for a few seconds.

"This here is Kole, Mr. Smith. He's training to be our new doorman." Hal nudged Kole forward by pushing lightly on his back—just enough to get Kole moving without making a scene.

"Well, nice to meet you, Kole. You have a great teacher here." James nodded toward Hal and walked into the building.

"He's a good man," Hal said as James walked to the elevators.

Halfway through the day, the doorman's kiosk rang. Hal picked it up. Usually it was one of the assistants informing him to watch for a dignitary that was either coming or leaving. This time it was Betty, Mr. Smith's assistant. "Hal, there's a meeting in a few minutes in the main conference room for all employees. Mr. Barnes is going to address us. There's not enough room, so they're filming it. You may want to find a television in the lobby and watch it. Things are about to change."

"Ah, all right. Thanks, Betty." Hal was confused by Betty's ominous tone. She was usually to the point. It piqued Hal's interest. In all his years he had never heard of Mr. Barnes ever doing a company meeting over the building's television.

"Kole, I need to go inside for a few minutes. Do you think you'll be all right out here?"

"Sure, Mr. Hal."

Hal knew that it was the slow time of the day, and if it was important enough for Betty to call down, then he wanted to see what Mr. Barnes was going to say. He found a small television set in the lobby that two security guards were watching.

The three of them watched Mr. Barnes step up to a microphone. Hal could see other executives standing solemnly behind him, including Miss Priar in her bright pink skirt.

"Hello everyone. It is with heavy hearts that we gather

you here today." *He's going to resign*, Hal thought. He had been a good boss, and Hal wasn't ready for a new one, not when he only had two years left.

"I wanted to tell you myself all at once, so there would be no rumors. As you are all aware, the economy has not been as strong in recent times. Near World has not been immune to the effects of a bad market. Our sales and shares have drastically declined. We have done all we can to keep the company afloat, but it has, to our dismay, come time to let some of you go. In order to keep Near World a healthy company we need to downsize, at least for the time being."

A rock dropped and hung in Hal's throat. What did he just say? They were firing people?

Mr. Barnes continued after the flurry of voices quieted. "Now, we don't know how many yet, but those who will have to say good-bye will be notified personally. I wish we didn't have to do this, but we do. None of us knows the future, and if the market comes back, I would hope those of you who leave would be willing to come back. I understand this is hard to hear. It is hard for me to say. I think of you all as family and wish it wasn't this way. Thank you." With that, Mr. Barnes stepped from the microphone and out the back door. The room erupted in noise. Hal watched in disbelief until the television went gray and fuzzy and eventually black.

They were cutting people. The first to go would be those deemed nonessential. Hal's fears of not being a good provider suddenly rushed back. A terrifying thought started ringing in his ears.

A doorman is not essential.

21

Halbert Germaine

Hal took his time going home that night. He didn't know what to tell Frances. What were they going to do? What about the house? What about the kids? They would have to quit school. Hal's world was crumbling around his feet just when he thought he had landed on solid ground.

The house smelled like fresh bread and meatloaf when he walked in the door. "He's home!" He heard one of the boys yell for everyone to come. They always waited for Hal to arrive before starting dinner.

Hal hung up his jacket and paused in the dark foyer for a minute to compose himself. He wanted to tell Frances first—before he told the kids.

He walked into the dining room where his three youngest children were already seated around the yellow laminate-covered table. Frances looked over at him.

"Hello, Daddy. Welcome home," she said, smiling warmly. Hal almost broke down right there. But he couldn't.

He made it through dinner and then sat at the table and watched Frances clean up. He couldn't move. Depression had rooted him to his seat.

After all the children had gone upstairs, Frances put away the last dish and sat in the chair next to him so she could see his face. She reached up and patted his right hand that was resting on the table. "Hal, baby, what's wrong? You haven't been yourself all night."

Hal looked up and couldn't contain himself any longer. "I'm gonna lose my job, Frances." He looked down, defeated. He felt Frances's hands tense up and pull away.

"What'd you mean, you gonna lose your job? What'd you do, Hal?"

"Nothin'. I didn't do nothin'. Mr. Barnes called a meeting today for all the employees to tell us the company is not doing well, and they need to cut back. He was nice about it and all, but if they cut back, I know I'll be the first to go."

Frances gasped and put her right hand over her mouth as she did when something worried her. She reached out again and squeezed his hand. "Hal, don't say that. You're the most loyal employee they got. You won't be first. You won't!"

She said it with so much conviction that Hal almost believed it. He had put twenty-eight years of his life into this job. They surely couldn't let him go that easily. Then reality struck again. "No, Frances, every one of them's got two hands and two arms. They don't need a doorman. No matter how much they like me, they can open the door for themselves. Most of them don't even know my name. They wouldn't know me from any other stranger on the street if I wasn't wearing a maroon suit and standing in front of their door." The truth was harsh, even for Hal. He had known it all along, but saying something so intimate out loud made him feel vulnerable.

Hal heard Frances snuffle and looked up to see her crying

as she shook her head in disbelief. "What're we gonna do, Hal? What're we gonna do? What about the mortgage and the boys' college?"

It broke his heart to see Frances shaken like this. Yet he couldn't do anything about it. All the confidence he had felt a few weeks ago on Rhonda's birthday had vanished. All he could manage was, "I don't know. I'm sorry, Frances. I'm so sorry."

22

Halbert Germaine

Hal went to work the next few days just as he had for years. He greeted all the Near World staff as if he hadn't heard Mr. Barnes's announcement. He figured that all of these people must be worried about their own jobs too, and it did no good to sit and mope about it. He would provide happiness as he always had for as long as they let him.

One afternoon it started to rain as everyone was leaving. Kole had gone home early for the day, and Hal waited for the last few stragglers to exit the building before going home. He watched from under his brass awning as frantic city dwellers ran to and fro trying unsuccessfully to stay dry.

"Well, I guess I won't be going to my car yet." Hal jumped to hear the voice beside him. He turned to see Mr. Smith.

"I'm sorry, Mr. Smith. I must've been distracted. I didn't get the door for you."

"Hal, it's fine. Rain is peaceful, isn't it? Do you mind if I join you?"

"It'd be my pleasure, Mr. Smith."

"Hal, I'll stay but only on one condition."

"What's that?"

"You need to stop calling me Mr. Smith. That sounds like my father. No, not even he went by something that formal. It sounds like my dead great-grandfather."

"All right, Mr. Smi—I mean, what do you want me to call you then?" Hal asked, baffled.

"James. James is fine."

"Okay, Mr. James."

James laughed out loud at Hal's version of his name. "I guess that's a start!" Hal watched as James shifted his gaze out to the water coming down stronger and stronger. "You know, Hal, my mother and grandmother loved thunderstorms. We used to go out in the summer under the large porch and watch the lightning light up the sky and feel the thunder penetrate our chests. I learned to love rainstorms." Hal listened in silence as James seemed lost in his own thoughts.

James finally said quietly, "It's been a long time since I spent the time to just watch a storm go by. Those were simpler days, weren't they?"

Hal didn't have the same love for rainstorms, but he knew what James was saying about the way life was without worries and fears. Totally different from now.

He looked closely at James and saw worry etched into the dark circles around his eyes. Obviously this layoff situation was also bothering the chief accountant.

James startled Hal out of his thoughts. "Hal, do you have children?" Hal was caught off guard. He had never been asked about his personal life by anyone during all his time at Near World, much less a high-level person like Mr. James.

James looked up when Hal did not answer right away.

"Ah, yes. We have five children. Well, they aren't children any more. Our baby is seventeen already."

James's eyes showed genuine interest to hear about Hal's children. "What are their names?"

With that, the two of them stood for almost an hour waiting for the storm to end. They told stories about their children and laughed so hard that they cried several times.

"Well, Hal, it has been great talking with you, but Molly and the kids will be waiting for me. And it sounds like Frances will be waiting for you too."

Hal was surprised that James was so candid with him and had even remembered Frances's name.

James turned to walk away and then stopped to turn back. "You're a good man, Hal. Thanks for sharing a rainstorm with me." Before Hal could answer, James walked toward the garage.

Hal knew that no matter what happened with the layoffs, people high in the offices above his door were not doing this lightly. Today he had learned more about a man he already liked.

23

Halbert Germaine

"*Hal! Did you* hear?" Kole's excited voice called over to him as he was coming up the sidewalk from helping someone to their car with some boxes. By this time, Hal had grown fond of Kole. After years of working by himself at Near World, he welcomed having someone to work with him. Kole was full of stories, most of them nonsense, but Hal would listen and laugh along.

"Hear what?" Hal asked, gearing up to hear another one of Kole's odd stories that he had read on the Internet the night before.

Kole beamed with pride to know he knew something Hal didn't—that didn't happen . . . ever. "Mr. Smith found a solution to Near World's problems! We won't have to be fired!"

"Whoa! Slow down, young one. What're you saying?"

"I said Mr. Smith found a way for us to keep our jobs."

Hal couldn't believe what he was hearing. He felt a small

flower of hope emerge, and he couldn't afford to let it bloom if Kole's story wasn't true. "How'd you know that?"

"They just called to tell you, but you weren't here, so they told me."

"They? Who's they?"

"I don't know. Some lady. She sounded old."

Hal lightly slapped Kole on the shoulder with the back of his hand. "Kole, the first thing I taught you was to know *everyone* that works in this building. That means everyone, including the old ladies on the phone." Despite being a bit frustrated with Kole's lack of message-taking skills, he smiled.

Kole didn't miss a beat. "Actually, *sir*, the first thing you taught me was to call everyone 'sir' and 'ma'am.' But why does it matter? The important thing is Mr. Smith is helping us keep our jobs."

"And how is he doing that?" Hal was still not sure Kole wasn't just playing some kind of prank.

"I don't know all the details. I can't remember. Something about a cut in pay for the boss and a vote—"

"Move over, Kole. I need to call an old lady to tell me something your red little head can't remember."

Kole laughed as Hal playfully pushed him to the side and headed for the phone at the doorman's kiosk.

He called Betty, sure that she had called down. Betty was aware of everything, and he and Betty had always kept each other up on all the gossip of the company. Betty was always especially happy to share good news from Mr. James's office because she always viewed his success as *her* doing. And many times it was.

It rang once, and Betty picked up in a fake sprightly tone. "James Smith's office. How may I help you?"

"Betty, it's me. What's going on? My partner can't seem to remember any details." Hal shot an exaggerated eye roll and a smile toward Kole, who was a few feet away listening in on the conversation.

Betty's voice instantly ditched the fake tone and got down to business. "James has proposed to Mr. Barnes and the rest of the board an alternative to laying people off." So it was true. Kole wasn't coming up with some elaborate hoax.

"How?" Hal blurted.

"Would you stop interrupting me? I haven't got all day. Do you want to hear or not?"

"Sorry, sorry. Yes, I want to hear." Hal conceded.

"It works like this, pretty simple actually. I wish I would've come up with it myself." Hal itched to point out that was the first time she had given credit to someone else but decided against it. Betty was not someone to push if you wanted information. She was not shy letting you know she had the upper hand. "He proposed that all the high-level officials take a ten percent pay cut until the recession was over, so they would have enough money to keep everyone on staff."

"They'd do that?" Hal asked before he could stop himself. Luckily, Betty agreed and didn't get angry this time.

"I know. That's what I thought too. But they're meeting today at three o'clock to discuss it, and all of them will vote."

Hal couldn't believe it. He knew Mr. James was special. Now everyone would know. Waiting to hear the verdict of the three o'clock meeting was like waiting for Christmas as a child. Hal had the restless jitters all morning. He knew that some senior people in the office wouldn't want to give up their salaries. They all knew the company could function better without the "extra baggage." They may not vote for Mr. James's option. He wanted to hope that they would do it, but until he heard for sure, he was keeping his own emotions under control.

Finally, after two agonizing hours of guessing, the

announcement was made that the plan had passed. Thanks to their decision, nobody would lose their jobs for now. Hal could feel the collective sigh of all the employees at work waiting to hear what had happened.

Hal couldn't wait to tell Frances. He almost broke the front door trying to get in faster than the latch would unlock.

"Frances! Frances!"

Frances came running into the living room with a worried expression and dish soap up to both elbows. "What is it, Hal? Are you all right?"

Hal ran over and lifted her up and twirled her around. "Mr. James did it! He did it!"

Frances slapped him on the chest. "Did what? What'd he do? Calm down, Halbert."

Hal laughed with glee. "He saved our jobs."

"What?" Frances's face registered the same feelings Hal had earlier: she wanted to believe, but didn't dare let herself yet.

"He set a plan for all the high-level officials to take a pay cut for a while, and that gave the company enough money to pay salaries so nobody gets laid off. I get to keep my job!"

Frances had tears in her eyes and wiped them with the bottom of her apron. "Bless that man. And bless all those that are sacrificing for us."

24

Molly Rillet

The sunlight was delicious to Molly's skin. It took all her effort to not drop her heavy biology book and lift her arms and face toward the beams of warmth that knit a blanket of solace. For a fleeting moment she forgot all about the small details, pressuring due dates, and hundreds of anatomy words she needed to memorize before her exam in the morning. All that mattered to Molly right then was soaking in nature's best cure—vitamin D.

Molly laughed to herself and opened her eyes to the busy campus around her. The thought of vitamin D brought her back to reality—medical school. She was in her last year of school to become a nurse practitioner.

She shifted the books in her arms and started to walk. Along with vitamin D, the sun's exposure also emitted ultraviolet rays that, after frequent exposure, could burst capillaries, causing the layers of the dermis to become red—a sunburn. If that occurred too often, those cells could begin to mutate into melanoma.

This education is destroying my simple pleasures, Molly thought as she walked to the library to study. The truth was, Molly loved learning how the world functioned. She found nature, and the body in particular, fascinating. Understanding how small, unnoticeable chemical reactions create life as people know it gave Molly satisfaction.

Molly loved this college campus. The fusion between the old gothic stone architecture and newer modern buildings gave the impression that she was literally walking through history. The library was her favorite building.

The "old wing" of the library had an ornate stone exterior, and the interior was accented with dark trim and solid towering shelves. The "new wing" was a square building with a flat roof, fashioned after a 1960s-era government building. The two wings were joined by a grand atrium-style foyer. Molly spent most of her time in the old wing. She liked that the tall shelves created small, hidden coves to study in without being bothered. Other students were more prone to gather in the newer, more expansive area.

Molly neared the large glass doors, and just as she went to open one of them, someone behind her called out, "Wait!" Molly stopped mid motion and turned to see who was talking to her. She saw a guy smiling and walking up with a handful of books. Her quick deduction classified him as the average college guy around campus. He had light-brown hair and was wearing tennis shoes, dark jeans, and a loose button-up yellow shirt.

"Wait, I'll get that for you." He hurried up the walkway toward her. Molly was more amused than anything. This guy had more books in his arms than she did. She stepped aside as he shifted his heavy load to open the door.

Laughing, Molly made a show of entering the door. "Thank you so much, sir. What a gentleman."

"You're welcome," he joined right in on her role-play

and did a mock bow as she passed. Unfortunately, that caused one of the books to topple off his stack and land haphazardly on the floor.

Molly bent down to pick it up and handed it to him. "You know, it may be easier to let me open the next door for you." She looked down at the book she had just picked up. It was written in a language that she didn't understand. Quizzically, she eyed the man. "You read other languages?"

"Not really." He was suddenly shy and reached out for the book. "I was bringing it to help a friend."

Molly was intrigued by his humility. Not many other college guys had that quality—actually not any that she could recall at the moment. She smiled as brightly as she could, trying to ease his embarrassment, "Well, I can see that there is more to you than the yellow shirt lets on."

He looked down at his shirt as if he had forgotten what he was wearing. Forgetting she was in the entrance of the library, Molly laughed out loud. Her voice echoed off the small room of windows between the two sets of library doors. Quickly, she covered her mouth to stifle the laughs. The guy also began to laugh. She was glad to see that he had loosened up again.

"Here, let me get this door for you." Molly opened the second set of glass doors into the library.

The guy went through as if in a gallant parade. "Well, I thank you, my fair lady."

Molly nodded her head and followed him through the doors. "Well, I'm going this way." She shrugged her shoulder toward the old wing. Then, lifting her biology books a bit for emphasis, she added, "I need to be ready for an intense exam next week." She assumed that he would be joining the other students in the new wing.

"Great! I'm going that way too," he answered brightly. Molly narrowed her eyes, deciding if he was instantly changing his plans to follow her. He looked genuine enough. "I'll walk with you for a ways. My friend is meeting me there."

"Okay." Molly turned, and they walked across the glass chasm toward the stone archway of the old building.

As they neared the entrance, Molly saw that her friend Trina was manning the information booth. Trina looked up from what was no doubt her cell phone to see them approach. "Hey, Trina." Molly called out, "It's good we aren't your boss or you'd be caught using your phone on the job!"

Trina's face went white, and she forced a nervous smile. "Hi, Molly. James." She nodded toward the guy in yellow Molly was walking with. She shot Molly a wide-eyed stare of incredulity.

"What?" Then it dawned on her that Trina had said her boss was another student who had worked in the library for a few years and been promoted. She turned to the guy beside her. "You're not Trina's boss . . . are you?"

He just smiled at her and raised his eyebrows in jest. "Oh, my . . ." She turned to her friend who was still trying to find a place to hide the phone that they all knew she had. "Trina, I'm so sorry," Molly stammered. Then she dashed off in embarrassment toward a quiet place to hide.

Molly tried hard to study over the next few hours. Every few minutes she was distracted by thoughts of the guy in yellow. At first she was still completely embarrassed at what she had done to Trina. As time went on, the experience became more humorous. What were the chances that she would walk in with Trina's boss? Then again, he *was* wearing a yellow shirt. Just like the yellow shirt she had seen Trina in over and over. "I'm such an idiot," Molly groaned to herself.

A few pages of anatomy lessons later, she found herself thinking of him again. She hadn't even asked him what his name was. "Stop it. You need to study," Molly chided herself. To switch gears, she pulled out her stack of handmade flashcards with names of body parts in Latin and English.

She flipped through the first two cards, trying to commit them to memory. James. His name was James. Trina had said it when she said hello to them both.

Finally after a few hours of forcing herself to study, Molly knew it was fruitless. She collected her stuff and went looking for Trina.

Trina wasn't at the information booth when Molly made it back to the glass foyer. Molly hoped it wasn't because James had fired her. The thought propelled her to pick up her pace. If Trina wasn't at work, she would be at her apartment.

Molly knocked on Trina's door. She could hear the music playing loudly inside. She knocked even louder. "Trina, I know you're in there. Open up."

The door opened slowly. Molly stepped in, and Trina headed back to her bed without saying anything. Molly didn't blame her for being mad. She hoped that Trina really hadn't lost her job.

Molly shut the door behind her and dropped the heavy load of books on an empty chair. It felt good to be rid of at least that weight. She walked over to the blaring music and turned it down.

"Trina, I'm so sorry. I didn't know he was your boss." Trina rolled over on her bed to face Molly. She didn't say anything for a few seconds, and Molly tried to decipher the look on her friend's face.

Molly and Trina had known each other for the last four years. They were randomly selected to be roommates as freshmen. Molly had tried out for the pep squad the next year and talked Trina into it too. They spent nearly every waking moment together. Molly had graduated with her bachelor's in biology and applied to several schools to get her nurse practitioner license. Against the advice of her mentor professors she had opted to stay at the same school instead of "diversifying her education." Trina was one of the reasons. She had become the sister Molly never had.

Trina finally shifted over on her bed, leaving just enough room for Molly to sit next to where she was lying. Relief rushed through Molly; it was Trina's way of saying she wasn't mad—at least not too mad. Molly sat down on the bed next to her friend and finally voiced the question that had been bothering her. "Did you get fired?"

Trina laughed and sat up. "No. James wasn't happy, but he's a good guy."

"He seemed like it."

"I was just lucky he was in a hurry for his meeting."

"Meeting?"

"Yeah, he volunteers a few hours a day to help international students with their English papers or something like that," Trina said, dismissing the conversation. She stood up and walked over to her closet.

Molly wasn't ready to be done with the conversation, though. "That makes sense," she said.

"What makes sense?" Trina's muffled response came from inside the closet where she was digging for something in the back.

"Well, when we met he dropped a book that was in a different language. I asked him if he spoke another language, but he said he didn't. He really volunteers?"

Trina jumped up with a pair of shoes. That must have been what she was searching for. "Why're you asking so many questions about my boss? You didn't seem so thrilled to stay and talk earlier today. You ran off like a scared rabbit."

Molly didn't answer. She wasn't sure why the guy had made an impression. She looked up to see Trina watching her with a mischievous smirk.

"You *like* him," Trina accused.

Molly laughed nervously. "I don't like him. I just met him today. I didn't even know his name until you said hello."

Despite what she was saying, Molly couldn't hide her smile. Something intrigued her about the semi-nerdy guy who still believed in chivalry, service, and humility. Having dated plenty of guys from the teams she cheered on, Molly was not accustomed to those qualities.

"Don't lie to me. You know I know you better than that. I can set you up," Trina said with finality. There was no backing down—once Trina had it in her mind, nothing was going to stop her. Molly wasn't sure she even wanted to try. Meeting James was beginning to sound more and more exciting.

25

Molly Rillet

"*You look beautiful.*" Molly turned around to see her mother and Trina come into her room where she was preparing for the biggest day in her life—her marriage to James. This day was one she had never planned. She had even fought the idea of being married for several years. Her dream was to have a career, to work in the medical field, and to help others.

James had changed all of that.

They had dated for what was the last year of both of their schooling. James was truly a gentleman. For the first several months, Molly wouldn't let herself believe that he was real. She knew that at some point she would find out he was hiding a dark side, but it never happened. He wasn't perfect by any means. He had plenty of quirks, but those were some of the reasons Molly liked him. He was himself. Always.

James had asked her to marry him after they had been dating for seven months. Molly took a few days to answer because she knew this was going to change her plans. Much to James's credit, he didn't give up. He gave her the time she needed, and she loved him even more for that. And here she was. In an hour she would become Molly Rillet Smith . . . she would be Mrs. Smith.

Molly turned back to the full-length mirror and saw her reflection. The flowing white dress gave her the feeling she was floating on clouds. Today she would marry James, her best friend.

"Molly, why are you crying? Stop it; your mascara will run." Her mother came over and patted her face with a napkin to stop the tears.

"I'm just happy. I never expected all of this."

Between Trina and her mother, Molly didn't have to do much. She stood there and her two attendants fussed over her as if she were the queen.

"All right, I'm going to find my place. The ceremony will begin soon. I'm so proud of you." Her mother kissed her on the cheek and stepped back. "You look beautiful." And then she hurried out the door.

"Ready?" Trina hooked her arm with Molly's. "Let's go. We have a chapel full of people waiting for us." They walked together until they saw her father.

"My little girl," he said, giving Molly a quick hug and then standing beside her. He would be the one to turn her over to James. Traditional? Yes, but Molly wouldn't have it any other way. Her parents were her support and strength. This day was perfect because they were here sharing it with her.

They walked a few steps into the ceremony room, and although it was full, Molly had eyes for only one person—her funny, chivalrous man. James stood there, steady as ever. Today was the beginning of their journey together. Molly couldn't wait to start.

26

Molly Rillet Smith

James and Molly's life fell into a wonderfully comfortable routine. Molly had graduated from nursing school with her nurse practitioner certificate.

James still wanted to finish his master's degree in accounting and finance, so Molly achieved her dream and started a career. She worked to support them while he was in school full-time. He had one more exam left, and then his two years would be done, and he could start working.

Their days were busy, and their evenings were spent doing things together—cooking meals, visiting museums, or just being at the house. Molly couldn't imagine her life any other way. She often found herself thankful for that day when James had opened the door for her at the library.

"Molly, I'll cook dinner tonight. What do you want?" James called from the kitchen.

She stood up to join James. "Well, that's a treat," she teased. James tried to take a few days a week to cook so

Molly wasn't doing it all the time. He would say, "You can't do it all. I have to help somehow."

They fixed a simple chicken and salad meal together and sat down to eat. "Molly, what do you think about moving into the city?"

Molly looked up from her food to see what James was really asking. His question came out of left field. She must have had a confused look on her face because he rushed on, "I mean, we wouldn't have to *live* in the city. We could live close, and I could commute."

"I guess I've never thought about it. Why? What're you thinking?" She could see that James was completely serious, so there was something behind his questions.

James took another bite and thought pensively for a few moments before answering, "Well, I applied for a job." James was taking this slowly, as if he was unsure of what he was saying.

"And?" The suspense was driving her crazy. She wasn't sure where this conversation was going.

"I applied for a job at the job fair lined up by the school. I was called in for an interview by a few of the companies, and one of them gave me a job."

"What? Why didn't you tell me all of this?" Molly was shocked to hear about him getting a job; she didn't even know he had gone to an interview.

James looked down at his plate, took a deep breath, and looked back up at her. "Sorry, Molly. I wasn't trying to hide it from you. I just didn't know if it would go anywhere. Honestly, with all of the people applying I never expected to be called, let alone get an offer."

"No, no. This is amazing. I didn't mean it was bad. I just wasn't expecting it. Tell me about it. Who gave you an offer?" Molly reached over to grasp his hand. She wanted to let him know that she was serious about not being upset.

"Near World."

"Near World, like the large import and export firm downtown?" Molly interrupted, sure she had misheard.

James finally smiled. "Yes. That's the one."

"James, I'm so excited. That's amazing." This time Molly stood up out of her chair and sat on his lap to give him a hug. She wrapped her arms around his neck and kissed him. "I would follow you anywhere. The city would work for both of us. We could both commute."

Little did Molly know that move was another beginning to a journey that she didn't expect.

Molly stood in the bathroom of their one-bedroom city apartment in disbelief. "How did this happen?" She couldn't sort out all the complex emotions she was feeling. She looked down at the small white stick that symbolized a drastic change in her life, in James's life, in their plans.

James had just started his job a few months earlier. Molly was beginning to feel like a leader in her position at the hospital. Pregnancy changed it all. How would they care for the baby? How could she be a mother? What would James say? He worried so much about making their lives comfortable. This revelation would throw him off balance for sure. The worries of the world clouded around the room.

However, Molly also couldn't deny the feelings of excitement too. She had a little being growing inside her. She gently placed her hand over her stomach as if protecting the life-form that she wouldn't even know was there if it weren't for the white stick on the sink. Well, that and the fact that the smell of cooking eggs made her want to hurl.

Molly was distracted at work the entire day. The smells of the hospital had never seemed so potent as they did lately.

Some of them that she had never noticed before made her feel nearly too nauseated to walk. She also sorted out a plan on how to tell James about the baby.

Molly decided to tell him with a card over dinner. She and James had always been able to talk, so a simple dinner conversation would make it easier. Having candles and flowers would let him know there was something special to talk about. If he was expecting something, she reasoned, he would be less shocked.

Molly couldn't help but become more and more excited. Even if James was stressed, she wanted to know what he would think.

Molly looked at the clock. James would be home in about fifteen minutes. She lit the candles on the table and checked the roasted chicken she had in the oven. Her nerves started to unravel a bit as the time slowly passed.

The front door creaked open. "Molly, I'm home."

Molly stayed in the kitchen. She wanted him to come in and see what she had prepared. "I'm in here," she called.

"Wow! It smells delicious in here . . ." James's voice died off as he walked around the corner to the kitchen and saw the dinner waiting. A smile grew on his face. "What's going on here?"

"A surprise," Molly replied coyly. "Come sit down. Dinner's ready."

"All right," James said, chuckling. "Are we celebrating?"

Molly pulled the chicken out of the oven and acted as if she hadn't heard his question. She didn't want to tell him yet.

"That looks amazing," James said, playing along with her.

"I hope it tastes good."

They ate and had a wonderful time. As Molly served the carrot cake she had bought at the corner bakery, she finally said, "James, I have a surprise."

James mockingly looked surprised. "I would've never guessed. And do I finally get to know what this surprise is?"

Molly took a deep breath. *Here it goes*, she thought.

"I'm pregnant." There—it was out. Now it was up to James to respond.

He sat still for a second, trying to register what she had said. Molly was about to say something because his silence was worrying her when he finally spoke up. "Are you sure?"

Molly hadn't realized she was holding her breath. She exhaled. "Yes. I took the test this morning."

"That's a surprise all right."

"I know. It was a shock to me too. But I have been really feeling . . ." How could she describe it to him? Sick? Off? Yes, that's a good way to describe it. "I've been feeling off lately. So I took the test. I'm still not sure how I feel about it. It's so unexpected."

James stood up, walked over to Molly, kneeled down on the floor next to her, and took her hands. "Molly, it'll be all right. This is something to be happy about." He kissed the back of her hand.

Molly was so thankful that James was taking it better than she thought he would. However, she still had her own worries. "What about our careers?" she blurted out. She knew she was really asking him, what about *her* career. How was she going to be a mother and have a career too?

James looked her in the eye and said, "Molly, we'll find a way to make it work." He leaned up and kissed her. When he gave her a hug, she felt the worry drain out of her like a whoosh of bad air. She could breathe again.

The next several months were packed with preparing for their baby to come. The hospital administration was willing to do everything they could to help Molly know her job would wait for a few weeks while she had the baby.

When the labor contractions started, Molly was stunned

how forceful they were. James was the calm in her storm of pain and worry. Luckily, the labor didn't last long. Within two hours of arriving at the hospital, their son, Jaden, was screaming with his fresh lungs.

They placed Jaden in Molly's arms after they had both been cleaned up, and Molly spent several minutes studying his perfect little features. He was hers. He was theirs. The intensity of the primal mother instinct was something Molly was unprepared for.

"James?" she called from the bed. He stood up from the vinyl chair in the room and came to her side. He used his finger to wiggle into Jaden's miniature hand. "James." Molly looked up from the baby to James. "I don't want to go back to work."

"Are you sure?" James knew she didn't want to give up her career.

"Yes, I'm sure. I don't want to let someone else care for my baby while I'm at work."

"Molly, you know that I support any decision you make. I told you that if you wanted to work, we would find a way. If you decide to stay home, that's fine too. It's your call. However, you gave birth only a few hours ago. Let's give it some time and see how you feel then."

Molly was grateful for her husband. Again. He was really going to let her choose. She knew he was right—she shouldn't make rash decisions the day she gave birth. But as she watched Jaden sleep, she knew that it was unlikely she would change her mind.

27

Molly Rillet Smith

Molly *never changed* her mind. Her decision over ten years ago to stay home with Jaden, she felt, was the best decision of her life—well, next to marrying James.

Having been so set on her career for so long, Molly was astonished at the satisfaction she received from caring for Jaden. He was her world. Entire decisions were made based around how it would change Jaden's life.

After quitting, Molly was given the option to cash in her 401K. Again, with people advising her not to do it, she cashed it in, and she and James used it for a down payment on a modest home in the suburbs that they could grow in.

The timing couldn't have been any better because three years later another baby made an appearance in their home—Natalee. Four years after Natalee came Noah, her baby. Their little family brought Molly so much joy. James was the most amazing father too. He would come home from work, and although she could tell he was tired, he would spend time with the children.

James decided to coach Jaden's baseball team. Molly watched as the experience put James on the edge of his comfort zone. He played sports in high school, but he wasn't sure he could coach. Molly remembered the night James was trying to decide.

"I don't want to let him down," James said, voicing his worry about failing Jaden.

Molly had walked over and wrapped her arms around his waist. "James, you'll be fine. You've never backed down before. Don't start now. Besides, it will be a bonding experience for you and Jaden."

James had done it, and even though they didn't win many games, Jaden and James both enjoyed the year. Life in the Smith household was always full of action and surprise—nowhere near perfect, but there was always love.

Today was a rough day. Molly just wanted to sit on the couch, lean her head back, and close her eyes for a few minutes. She forgot how hard it was to have a three-year-old. Compounding the realities of the never-ending energy of Noah was the fact that she had Natalee home sick today too.

Molly was lethargic; she felt like she was swimming in sand and couldn't move fast enough to keep up. The house was a mess; she had alternated all day between a crying little girl and a toddler that wanted constant attention.

Thankfully James would be home in a few hours. Both children were in their rooms for a nap. Molly walked into the living room and saw the toys and clothing strewn around resembling a hurricane that had recently passed through. She knew she should use these brief moments to tidy up, yet she couldn't do it. She succumbed to her desire and sunk into the comforts of the couch. Just as she closed her eyes she heard a tiny voice call down the hallway: "Mommy!"

Molly stayed perfectly still, hoping Natalee would fall back asleep. There was silence again for another few minutes.

Molly relaxed again into the cushions. "Mommy!" This time it was louder. Molly groaned and stood up. If Natalee kept yelling she would wake Noah—then she would have both children crying. Dealing with one crying child was better than dealing with two.

"Yes, sweetheart. What do you need?" Molly asked as she entered her daughter's room. Natalee watched with big brown eyes.

"My head hurts," Natalee weakly whined.

Molly sat on the bed and caressed Natalee's face. Her skin was hot; she must still have a fever. Molly brushed back a few stray locks of hair. "All right. I'll be right back with some medicine." With a soft kiss on Natalee's cheek, Molly quietly left the room.

As she rounded the corner, she saw James in the kitchen. It was too early for him to get home. "You're home early," she said. He turned around, and Molly could tell he was having a hard day by just the look on his face. Alarmed, she walked over to him. "Are you okay?"

He pulled her into a hug and sighed. "Yes. I'm all right. It was an interesting day at work."

Molly took a deep breath. She loved to be close to James. She always felt safe and secure while she had her face against his chest and could feel his warmth. "By interesting, you mean bad?" she prodded.

"It depends on how you look at it."

Molly released her hug and stepped back so she could see his face. "Did something happen?" She fought to keep the protective panic out of her voice. For the last several months, James had been dropping hints that Near World wasn't doing as well as they had been. In a moment of in trepidation she assumed he had been laid off. "Were you laid off?"

James dropped his eyes to avert her stare, and Molly's body was paralyzed with a jolt of anxiety. She waited to hear his answer. She was also unsure what to say. For the first time in a long time she was scared. He finally cleared his throat—this was obviously making him emotional. "No, I didn't lose my job. Thankfully nobody did, but I took a pay cut."

Molly wasn't following what he was saying. "You what?"

James shook his head and was about to reply when Natalee's voice called, "Mommy!" Molly had completely forgotten why she had come to the kitchen in the first place.

She moved quickly to the cabinet for the medicine and gave James a light squeeze on his arm as she passed. "Natalee has a fever. Hold this conversation—I'll be right back."

He stepped up to her. "I can give her the medicine." He took the bottle of liquid out of her hand and grabbed a spoon from the drawer. Molly watched her husband quietly as he started out of the room. She wanted to comfort him, but her own thoughts were a mess.

A pay cut? How were they going to handle it? With three growing children, they were already living on the edge of their financial capacity. Her exhausting day was wearing her thin.

James turned back just as he reached the doorway. "I'm sorry, Molly." His voice was so full of emotion, it brought tears to her own eyes. James turned and walked down the hall to their daughter.

Molly sat down at the kitchen table, still unable to comprehend what James had said. She was worried enough that trying to do something productive was fruitless—she couldn't concentrate. She waited until she heard his footsteps returning.

Without a word, James put the medicine back into the cabinet and the spoon into the dishwasher. He walked over and sat kitty-corner from her. Molly reached for his hand over the table. She just waited for him to talk.

"Molly, I'm so sorry. I know this is going to put us in a horrible position financially. I never meant for this to happen."

Molly tried to keep the quavering out of her voice. "James, stop apologizing and just tell me what happened."

James took a long exasperated sigh. "It all happened so fast. It is still a bit shocking to me." He paused as if collecting his thoughts, and Molly waited patiently. "You know that Near World has been struggling for the last year. Mr. Barnes has his entire board working to keep the company moving forward. His goal was to not effect any layoffs. After trying for months and months, he and the board realized the numbers just weren't adding up. We had some long, heated conversations about it, and the decision was finally made that we had to let people go."

Molly was hit with anxiety again, followed by a selfish respite knowing her husband hadn't been one of the ones cut.

James continued, "Mr. Barnes announced to the whole company two days ago that the layoffs would start next week."

"What? Why didn't you tell me?" Molly was reminded of the last time this happened, when James had been offered this job.

"I know. I should've said something last night, but I was too saddened by it all to talk about it." James's averted his eyes, and a wave of sympathy spilled over Molly. "Yesterday, our first meeting was with the entire board to discuss which positions we deemed unnecessary. I could tell that all of them were having just as hard of a time as I was."

"I'm sure. Nobody wants to decide who gets cut."

"Then I spoke up. It was just a fleeting thought. I never expected anyone to take it seriously, let alone carry it out."

"What? Say that again." Molly was trying to grasp what he was saying.

"It occurred to me while I was looking around the room with all the high-level officials that if we all took a pay cut, there may be enough money to cover the salaries of the employees who may lose their jobs. I said it out loud, and before I knew it I was tasked to join in with a team of two other board members to work the numbers."

"And?"

"And it looked like it would work. Mr. Barnes called all the executive leadership together and surprisingly, after my presentation of the results, there was a resounding approval. Within two hours, a formal announcement went out to the entire company about the decision."

"James, that's great! You saved all those people's jobs." Molly was sincerely impressed with her husband.

"Yes, I'm happy that we didn't have to cut anyone." Then he became serious again. "Molly, a ten percent pay cut is destructive to our own household. We're already living pay check to pay check. Mr. Barnes and people like Susan Priar can afford to take a ten percent pay cut with their salaries. I'm just the accountant."

Molly could see why James was worried. James had just voiced her own concerns, yet she was still full of gratitude for her husband's giving and caring nature. He had saved so many families. Yes, it would be hard, but they could make it. "James, what you did is amazing. You and those board members did the right thing. It may be hard, but we can make this work."

James smiled, a weary unconfident smile. "I hope so. I hope it can all work out. I can't defeat the feeling that I sacrificed the happiness of my own family."

"I'm proud of you, James."

He pulled her over for a hug. "Thanks, Molly. I hope that I did the right thing."

28

Molly Rillet Smith

It was a beautiful spring day. The grass was shedding its brown coat in exchange for a succulent green. Fireworks of color filled the flowerbeds along the streets of their neighborhood. More than anything else, though, the restlessness of the children proved it was time to leave the weary cold behind and embrace summer.

The phone rang, and Molly, in the adjacent laundry room folding some of the never-ending laundry pile, heard Jaden pick it up in the kitchen. "Hello?" After a short pause he said, "Hold on for a moment. I'll go get her." Molly was happy to hear that her lessons to Jaden and Natalee about phone etiquette were being absorbed. A few seconds later, Jaden arrived at her side with the cordless phone in his hand. "It's Jessica."

Molly took the phone from Jaden. "Thank you, bud." Jessica was a friend Molly had made shortly after moving to the suburbs. Jessica lived only a few blocks away and had children around the same age as Molly and James's. The two of them often planned activities for their kids together. Much like Trina during college, Jessica had become like a sister to her. She put the phone up to her ear. "Hello?"

Jessica's cheerful voice greeted Molly. "Molly, my kids are driving me crazy. Is there something we can do with them today?"

A chuckle escaped from Molly. "You too? I was trying to decide how to appeal to the school for no more days off."

"I know, right?" Molly could hear Jessica laughing too.

"James bought a small kid's pool the other day. We could fill it up in the backyard and let the kids run wild."

"Sounds like a plan. But I'm sure Mr. Scheimer won't be as excited as we are."

Molly burst out laughing as Jessica mentioned their elderly neighbor. More than once over the last ten years, Mr. Scheimer had growled at the children for being noisy or kicking a ball into his manicured roses. "You're right. But I'm still not convinced he doesn't enjoy it." Jessica and Molly had a faux bet whether Mr. Scheimer would come out and sit on his deck when the children were running in the yard to protect his bushes and territory, or if he liked having the distraction.

"In that case, we'll be over in a few minutes."

Molly hung up and called down the hall. "Jaden, Natalee!"

Natalee was the first to arrive at the laundry room door. "Yeah, Mom?" Her hair was in a crooked ponytail off the side of her head. Natalee had recently decided she would learn how to do her own hair. So far her attempts were unsuccessful.

"Jessica is coming over with her kids to play in the pool outside. Do you want to put on your suit and help Jaden fill the pool up?"

The effect was instantaneous. "Yeah!" Natalee took off

running before Molly could suggest that she fix her hair. "Jaden! Mom said we can fill the pool!"

Molly laughed.

Jessica and her kids arrived, and soon the backyard was reverberating with squeals of delight. Molly and Jessica settled into two Adirondack chairs on the porch. They both positioned their chairs to maximize the exposure to the soft rays of the sun.

"How long do you think it will take?" Jessica asked. Molly looked over at Jessica, confused at her question. Jessica had her face turned up to the sun and her eyes closed.

"For you to get tan?" Molly joked.

Jessica sputtered a laugh. "No. For Mr. Scheimer to come out."

Molly glanced over at his deck to see if he had appeared yet. "I'm not sure. With all this noise, it can't be too long." Sure enough, as if he had heard them talking, the back door of Mr. Scheimer's house opened, and he shuffled out to a chair in the sunshine.

"There he is." Jessica was also watching him. They watched until he settled in a chair from which he could watch the two yards. Jessica finally turned to Molly again. "How're you doing, Molly?"

"Fine. Why do you ask?" Molly's answer was immediate, too quick to be a real answer.

"Come on, Molly. How are you doing, really? You've seemed tense the last couple of days."

Molly knew she couldn't keep hiding from Jessica. They knew each other too well. "I'm worried." Jessica didn't respond, just sat and waited for more explanation. Then, once Molly started, it was like a deluge of information. She told Jessica about James's decision at work, about the cut in pay, and how it was going affect their finances. "I'm afraid it may stretch us too thin," she added lamely in conclusion.

Jessica, a good listener as always, waited for a few moments to respond. "Molly, I can see how that would worry you." They both turned to watch as a fresh wave of screams came from the yard. Jaden had started spraying everyone with the hose. "Have you ever considered going back to work? Even part time?"

Molly looked back at Jessica. "I would love to be back at work. It would relieve some stress off James. But it would be hard to leave Noah with someone I don't know."

"What about part time? I could take Noah for a few hours a day. I have Kally anyway, and it would be good for them to have each other when all the older kids are at school."

"You would do that?" Molly could feel the reels of her mind making plans for this to work.

"Of course I would. You know I love your kids like my own."

"Let me think about it . . . and talk to James. That may be a great idea."

The more Molly thought about working again, the more she liked the idea. She would have to run it by James when he came home.

When James walked in the door, the regular barrage of greetings came from the children. Molly found herself suddenly nervous. Was her plan foolish? She opted to wait and tell him later in the evening. That would give them time to talk without the children and, more important, give her time to think it through more thoroughly.

That moment came as James was helping her clean up the dishes. All three children were already in bed. Molly knew she needed to just say it—get it out before she lost her nerve. "James, what do you think about me going back to work?"

"What? Where did that come from? I thought you liked being home with the kids." James looked over at her while he put away a few dishes he had just dried.

"I do love it. But I also miss my career, and I feel like with your job . . ." She stuttered over how to put it. ". . . with the situation with Near World, that I could go back part time, and it would help out."

James had stopped drying dishes and was watching her. Molly perceived a hint of hurt in his face. "Molly, I don't expect you to do that."

"I want to, James. I miss working," she assured him.

"What about the kids?"

"Jaden and Natalee go to school. I can be home before they are done for the day."

"And Noah? Who will care for him?"

Molly was thankful she already had an answer for that question. "Jessica said she would watch him while I was at work."

James paused, apparently trying to decide how he felt about it. "Molly, as I told you many times, I will support any decision that you make. I just don't want you to do this because of the pay cut."

"James, it's unfair to say that. I have been thinking about work for years. I miss the medical field beyond kissing bruises and scrapes better. I know you support me. You always have. That's one of the things I love about you—you never dictate what I do. Your pay cut just gives me an incentive to start working again." She stopped talking and watched him. She wished he didn't look so defeated.

"All right. If you think it will work, we can try it out. But if you ever decide it's not working for you, you need to quit. We'll find another way."

She walked across the kitchen to give him a kiss. "Thank you, James. Thank you for giving it a chance."

He gave her a hug. "I just hope this salary cut is only temporary." Molly chose not to respond. She knew that must be his pride trying to justify his wife having to go back to work.

29

Molly Rillet Smith

The hospital had been more than happy to welcome Molly back to their ranks. Molly found that even after ten years, the medical practice came back naturally. She had to be honest with herself: the first two weeks were hard. Every time she left Noah at Jessica's she had to fight the feelings that she was abandoning him—giving up.

It almost made her feel guilty when she realized how much she liked work—was she becoming a bad mother? She had voiced the concern to Jessica one day. She didn't dare tell James; she knew he would've leaned on her to quit. She wanted to at least give it a few months before making a decision.

Jessica had responded, "Molly, you love your job. There's nothing wrong with that. In fact, I'm glad that you do."

Jessica was right. Noah adapted to his scheduled quickly. Molly could see that he even liked being around Kally while Molly was at work.

Since then their home had taken on a new dynamic. She had relaxed knowing the finances were available, and although her most important duty in life was being a mother, she found satisfaction in her career.

It was James she worried about. He never seemed to get used to the idea of her working. He would drop hints here and there that he had, in some way, failed her by not letting her have the choice to go back—she had to go back by necessity.

Molly stopped in front of Jessica's house. "All right, you're here." She and Jessica had worked it out that Molly would pick up all of their elementary school kids after work and bring them home while picking up Noah. Molly watched as Jessica's older children said their good-byes and ran into the house.

She saw Jessica chasing a bouncy little Noah out the door with his backpack in her hand. He insisted that he take his backpack wherever he went. Inside of it he had a few toys, and Molly used it to her advantage and put in a few diapers and wipes too. As they arrived, Molly stepped out of the car and bent down. Noah jumped right up into her arms, nearly knocking her over.

"Mommy!"

His love was infectious. "Hey, little guy. Did you have a good day?"

"MMM-mm," was his reply as she stood up with him in her arms.

"Wow, you are getting heavy. Mommy won't be able to carry you much longer."

Noah beamed proudly. "I's a big boy."

"Yes, you're a big boy, all right. Just like your brother, Jaden."

Noah's brow knit in thought, and he said with a very serious tone, "No. I not big like Jaden."

Both Molly and Jessica, who had caught up to them, laughed. "No, you're not. You're right. Jaden is still your big brother." She turned to address Jessica. "How did he do?"

"Fine as always." Jessica smiled and handed her Noah's backpack. "Oh, and here are the new words you ordered." Jessica had joined the fad of vinyl lettering on the walls and there were a few sayings that Molly wanted.

"Perfect timing. Thank you again for everything."

"Anytime. See you tomorrow," Jessica cooed back to Noah, who was now buckled into his seat. "Hello, Jaden. Hello, Natalee," she greeted the other two in the car.

Molly put up the words as soon as she arrived. The first was a large black lettering that read: FAMILY. She placed it on the wall in the living room just above their family photos. The second was more personal. She walked back to the mirror in the bathroom and carefully applied the words at the top. She stood back and admired it. This was one that she had felt inspired to get.

The sentence read: YOU MAKE A DIFFERENCE.

Molly had chosen these words for James. She had watched him go through a hard time recently, and she wanted him to know that he made a difference in people's lives. She hoped it would help. After confirming that the quote was adhered correctly, she rushed off to cook dinner.

Molly watched at the end of the evening to see when James went back to the room. She wanted to be there when he saw the quote. It was well after the children had gone to bed that they both made it to their room.

"How was your day, James?" Molly realized with the craziness of the family she hadn't asked him about his day.

"Okay. Same old work and meetings . . ." James stopped mid-sentence as he walked into the bathroom and looked at the mirror. Molly waited for him to say something; he stood there in silence for several minutes.

She walked over and leaned on the door. "Are you all right?" He was just staring at the mirror.

"Yes," he said and then continued to prepare for bed. Molly wanted to cheer him up; something was obviously bothering him.

The first thing she thought of was his birthday coming up. "Hey. What are we going to do for your birthday? It's a big one." James was turning forty in a few weeks.

James grunted. "Nothing. Birthdays are just another day now."

That didn't work. She dropped the line of conversation and moved on to more safe topics. As they climbed into bed, Molly lay awake long after James had fallen asleep. James was clearly still bothered by something. He just didn't see the amazing person that he was. What could she do to show him how much they all appreciated him?

Then the thought occurred to her. She could throw him a surprise party for his birthday. Molly knew he would never consent to it if she asked him about a party, so a surprise party was the only way to go. She would ask everyone to bring a short note or say a few words about how James had helped them in their lives.

Yes. That was it. Molly would start the planning in the morning.

30

Gerald Scheimer

"He's late." Gerald grumbled at the old grandfather clock that stood in the corner of the living room. Beside the clock was a matching wooden shelf full of family photos and military memorabilia from Gerald's thirty-year career in the military.

If there was one thing Gerald had learned from his time in the military, it was to be punctual. "There's no excuse for tardiness!" he used to yell in the faces of fresh recruits. "It is only a sign of laziness, and a lack of proper preparation."

Even now, at the age of eighty-five when all his bones ached and his skin drooped, he couldn't tolerate when people were late. Gerald stood up awkwardly, using his walker and the arm of his favorite chair to stand himself up. He shuffled his feet over to the door, oxygen tank in tow, in anticipation of the arrival. "He should be here by now."

These young kids thought they knew everything, with their fancy gadgets, big houses, and new cars—they were sure the older generation was missing something. Gerald knew they were wrong. All the gadgets in the world couldn't make up for a foundation of respect, honor, and hard work.

Gerald opened his door and stood at the glass storm door, watching. He saw the two children dash out of the house to the car. Gerald harrumphed. "Spoiled brats. In my day we never had a horse, much less a car to take us to school and back. All we had were our two little feet." Even as he thought this, Gerald knew that part of him was jealous of the nimbleness and litheness of the two children.

Finally Gerald saw James exit the house next door. He opened the car door and threw in his black work-bag, then jogged swiftly over to the newspaper that the lazy newspaper man had left on the sidewalk. James bent down and swooped up the paper without even slowing.

As he neared, Gerald opened his storm door. "You're late again."

James smiled kindly enough and dismissed the comment. "Good morning, Mr. Scheimer. I hope you have a good day. It looks like it'll be a nice one." He held the paper out toward Gerald. Gerald reached out and grabbed it. He went to say something else, something nice—something to keep him there talking for a few minutes. But James was already halfway down the sidewalk jogging back to his waiting children in the car.

And just like that, it was over. The most contact Gerald had all day with someone not over a phone had come and gone in two short minutes. Gerald stepped back and shut the door. He pulled back the curtain just far enough to see James pull out of his drive and speed up the lane.

He looked at the newspaper in his hand. He might as well start his daily routine. Each day was exactly the same. He read the paper while eating his toast. He used to have coffee with it, but the doctor told him coffee reacted badly with his medicine. Now he just drank milk.

Gerald poured some milk into his mug that displayed the great seal of the ship he had called home for several months during World War II. In the days, or years, that he spent training new soldiers, surrounded by people who worked under him and respected him, he never expected to come to a point in his life where he would live in a big house in the suburbs all by himself.

Gerald was accustomed to being at the top of his game. Now he felt like an old dusty artifact on a shelf, long forgotten and replaced.

He spread out the paper before him. The toast was dry as always, and he took the five pills that were designated for morning. When did he cross the line that he took more pills than the number of people he talked to in the day? Gerald reached into his shirt pocket for his reading glasses.

"Dag-nabbit!" They weren't there. He must have left them in the room where he had been reading last night. Gerald stared down at the blurry pages of the newspaper. He would have to get his glasses to make sense of any of the mess before him. He stood up and walked slowly back to his bedroom.

By the time Gerald had reached the hallway, his cough had returned. "Stupid cough." Gerald yelled out between fits. He reached out to the wall for support as his body shook violently.

When he was done, he pulled out his hanky to wipe the spittle that had escaped and was now drooling down his chin. He then wiped his head, which was beginning to bead with sweat.

Gerald looked at the bookshelf across the hall from him. Each shelf was filled with artifacts and photos from different chapters of his life. There were photos of him with his parents when he was a child. They were old, grainy, and unclear, but it was the last memory of his mother's face that he had.

There were also more recent photos of his two children, Vicki and Robert, with their families. These two children were his pride and joy. Sadly, he had missed so much of their younger years because he was too focused on his career. His wife, Grace, had raised them.

Later Gerald regretted the birthdays, the ball games, and the family moments he had missed. But it was too late. At best his relationship with his children was cordial. They were kind and loving, of course, but their love was stronger for Grace. Grace's passing had only exposed the ugly rift between him and his children that, for years, they had all pretended wasn't there.

Gerald continued into the bedroom. This was not the bedroom that he and Grace had shared. It was actually meant to be an office. Although the home was two stories and a basement, Gerald only used the main floor these days. He didn't have the energy to climb the stairs.

Winded, he sat on the bed. Sure enough, his reading glasses were sitting on the small table next to a cordless phone and a gold-framed glamour photograph of Grace from the year they married.

Gerald tenderly picked up the photo. "Grace, my love, I'm not the man I once was. I'm a broken old grouch. And I am living in a shell of a house too quiet to be a home." Gerald brought the photo up to his lips and kissed it tenderly. "I miss you, Grace."

Placing the photo back, he grabbed his glasses and went back to the kitchen to finish his breakfast.

Gerald looked at his watch. It was gold-faced with worn leather; he had worn it for years. It was time for the news. He settled into his oversized recliner and turned on the television. He always liked to keep up on current events, but he watched the two o'clock news for a different reason too—schedule. Parts of his military background never retired.

Having a schedule gave him purpose—if anyone asked, Gerald himself would admit that it was false purpose, but it helped nonetheless.

The other reason Gerald liked the schedule, and consequently the toast and milk breakfast and the two o'clock news, was that it helped the day move along. The ticking of the grandfather clock was a constant reminder that the house was too quiet. The days droned on, one tick at a time.

Gerald had contemplated selling the clock several times, but it was one of Grace's favorite pieces in the house, and he hoped that at some point either Robert or Vicki would take it to remember their parents.

The only respite from the monotony was the routine caring for his garden and the family next door. Whenever Gerald heard the children in the yard playing, he would open the window so their laughter could fill the empty walls with color. Or he would walk out and sit on his own deck to watch them play. In his mind he would envision his own children in them. The moments he had missed, he lived vicariously through James and Molly.

James and Molly had always tried to include Gerald in their neighborhood parties, family dinners, and summertime barbecues. Gerald accepted some invitations, and others he turned down. His pride wouldn't allow him to appear as lonely as he truly was. He didn't want to be seen as a beggar at their door.

He had watched James with his children, and part of him was jealous that James was spending the time with his children that Gerald never had. He made sure to point out whenever the children were disobeying and needed some discipline. Although Vicki and Robert had never learned to love him, they had learned how to respect people and property. Another thing this younger generation of parents failed to teach.

The phone rang, and Gerald opened his eyes. He must've fallen asleep. He quickly rubbed the drool off his face with his sleeve. Groggily he fumbled with the channel changer to mute the blaring television. The news was long over, and some immoral modern show was playing.

The phone rang again. Gerald pulled his recliner closed and stood up slowly. His body just didn't want to wake up yet. "I'm coming!" he yelled at the impatient shrieking from the wall phone in the kitchen. It rang four more times as he pushed his walker as fast as he could.

In his head, he coaxed the caller, *Don't hang up, don't hang up. I'm almost there.* He finally reached the phone and grabbed it off the wall, the exertion triggering his cough.

"Hello . . ." he managed to say into the receiver before a fit came rumbling out of his lungs. He tried to use his shaking left hand to cover the receiver as he coughed.

"Dad? Are you all right?" It was Vicki's voice.

Gerald tried to answer, but the more he tried to stifle his cough, the worse it got. He flopped into a kitchen chair and let his lung seizure subside. Finally he could answer. "Hey, Vicki." He wiped the spittle on his face again.

"Dad, that sounds horrible. Are you all right?"

Gerald cleared his throat. "I'm fine. How're you? How are the kids doing?"

"Dad. Stop trying to change the subject. How long have you been coughing like that? Does your doctor know?"

Gerald became annoyed at all of her questions. He hated when people pointed out his weaknesses—he had always hated it. Getting old wasn't easy for Gerald. Having to ask for help—needing help at all—and experiencing all of the weaknesses of being elderly only angered him. Aging and pride are the same side of two magnets repelling each other and being forced together.

"I'm fine," he growled. Immediately he regretted his

tone. This wasn't winning him any points with his daughter. She made sure that she called every day to check on him. "Thanks for calling, Vicki. How are the kids?"

"They're fine, Dad. They're growing up. I wish you would take my offer and come here for a few weeks so you could see them."

Vicki and her husband, Sam, had asked Gerald to come stay with them several times. He always turned them down. He didn't want to be a burden, and it was too embarrassing to let them see all of the attention that he needed just to do normal daily functions.

"I would love to see them, but it's too far of a trip." That was his standard answer.

"I know, but you're welcome anytime if you change your mind. How are Molly and James doing?" Gerald would often tell Vicki about going over to the neighbors, and she usually asked about them.

"They're all right. I talked to James this morning on his way to work." Although untrue, he didn't want Vicki to know how lonely he truly was.

The conversation with Vicki was short, and when he hung up Gerald looked at the grandfather clock. It was time in the schedule to start getting ready for bed.

31

Gerald Scheimer

I*t took Gerald* several hours to get ready in the morning. Shaving, showering, and dressing were all physically exhausting ordeals that required frequent rests. For this very reason he would wake up at a quarter to five. He had to be ready before seven. James usually left the house any time between seven thirty and seven forty-five. It was his one chance to have someone to converse with; he wasn't going to miss it.

Gerald finished showering and was pulling on his socks. It was hard to bend down to his feet. For years he took for granted the ability to do small acts like dressing himself. The labor required to put on just one sock forced Gerald into another coughing fit. He had to stop for a few minutes and wait for the coughing to pass. The entire bed shook with his convulsions. His cough finally quit but left him gasping for air.

Slowly he started putting on his other sock. The last part

of the dressing process was his shoes. He tied his laces and headed down the hall. He would wait in his recliner until it was closer to seven thirty. Just as he rounded the corner of the hallway, the clock chimed one deep chime, signifying it was half past the hour. Instead of heading to the chair, he went straight for the door.

When he opened it, James was already heading up to the door. "Good morning, Mr. Scheimer." He handed Gerald the paper and dashed off in a hurry.

Gerald watched James retrace his steps to his car. "Thank you," Gerald said quietly to the crisp morning air as James and his children drove off to their day.

Several times Gerald looked at the clock. Even his routine wasn't distracting enough. There were still two more hours until the two o'clock news. Gerald refused to watch other shows. They were all trash in his opinion. He began to track how long he could go between coughing fits. It was becoming more and more frequent. His entire body was in pain. All those wretched pills, and they weren't helping anything.

There was a soft rap on the door. Gerald held his breath; he wasn't sure if he had heard something or if his mind was playing tricks on him. A few seconds later he heard the soft rap again.

Who could that be? Nobody came to visit him, especially at this hour. He started the work of standing and yelled, "Coming. Give me a minute to get there." He didn't want someone to think he wasn't there and leave.

When he opened the door, he saw Molly. She was dressed in her hospital clothes. "Hello, Mr. Scheimer. I'm off to work, but I wanted to bring this over." She held out a paper about half size to him. "We're having a surprise party for James's fortieth birthday next week. We'd love it if you could come."

Gerald took the invitation. "Thank you. I'll see what's on my schedule. Next week you say?"

Molly chuckled politely. "Yes, next week, Mr. Scheimer. I hope you can pencil it in. Have a great day." She smiled again. "I need to be off now. I don't want to be late for work."

"Good-bye!" Gerald called out as she walked back to her house.

He stood there, staring out into the street for several minutes before shutting the door. Molly's kind words and invitation were worth more than all the medicine in the kitchen put together. He looked down at the invitation. He knew, and he knew Molly knew, he didn't have anything on his schedule. Molly and James had just given him something to look forward to.

Gerald shuffled into the kitchen. He took the paper Molly had given him and straightened it. He cursed himself for wrinkling it on the walk over. "Blasted walker anyway."

Once he was convinced it was as smooth as he could get it, he placed it on the fridge with a magnet proudly painted by Robert years ago at summer camp.

The words, "Come to a Surprise Birthday Party for James!" glared happily back at him. Today had turned out to be a good day after all.

32

Lanie Smith Dorne

L*anie stared down* at the photo on her smartphone screen. The couple staring back at her was young and full of love. They had lofty dreams of finishing school and starting a family together. They had spent hours and hours conceptualizing their future—the house they would live in, the number of children they would have, the places they would travel. Lanie sadly pushed the button to turn her screen off. As the black replaced the colorful photograph, she thought how that couple had no idea how hard that journey would become.

She had married Dan Dorne nearly five years ago. He was everything to her. He still was. They had dated for nearly a year before deciding to get married. Every day he filled her life with laughter and joy. Lanie still recalled the day that she brought Dan home from college to meet her family.

It was a cold February break. She and Dan had driven

through a horrible snowstorm to get there. Lanie couldn't decide if her nerves were due to the icy roads or the impending meeting with her family. They all knew she was coming with Dan, and therefore, all four siblings and their families—the ones that were married anyway—came for a family dinner. Lanie loved her family, yet all at once she knew they could be a bit . . . overbearing.

They were a loud and opinionated bunch. Lanie was the fourth in seniority—only her baby sister Sierra was younger, and thankfully unmarried. Lanie didn't want to be known as the last one single. Sierra was several years younger than Lanie, and nobody in the family could deny that she was the shining star in their parents' eye; although, if you asked them they would surely deny it. Of her three older siblings, she was closest to James.

James was a year older than she was. For some reason the two of them had bonded when they were really young, and that bond remained strong today. Maybe it was a result of them being so close in age, or a necessity. Her two older siblings, Paul and Olivia, claimed much of the spotlight as they were growing up. The discarded remains were shared by Lanie and James.

Lanie loved her parents dearly, and she knew that they loved each of them too. It wasn't their fault, Lanie knew; it was only a circumstance of their situation. Having five children, all close in age and growing up in the same household, required both of them to work. They spent hours and hours slaving to make ends meet. Lanie was thankful for them, although even now she was not sure she understood the sacrifices they went through.

With every mile that Dan drove, Lanie's nerves stretched tighter until she figured that if they were plucked with a finger they would give a shivering high pitch. She reached over and placed her hand on Dan's leg. Knowing he wasn't worried comforted her. He could be hiding it, for all she knew, but it comforted her nonetheless.

Molly, James's wife, had called to say that she and James would be there tonight. That thought was a small gift. At least she knew James would stick up for her, as he always had. Lanie laughed at herself. What was she thinking? Her family was not the mafia. She was just bringing a guy home.

"What?" Dan asked her when she laughed.

She reached up and squeezed his arm, taut from gripping the wheel. "They're going to love you."

"I hope so. We need to make this drive worth it." Dan grinned back.

Lanie was right; they did love Dan. Surprisingly, for once, Lanie was the center of the evening. Even Olivia and Paul focused on Lanie and Dan. Lanie wondered if this was what life as adults would be like—all of them equals. Nothing brought more joy to Lanie, though, than to see that James and Dan were able to strike up an immediate friendship. It would have bothered her to know that two men so close to her didn't like each other.

That had been five years ago.

Lanie looked up from her blank phone screen and watched for Dan to come out of his work building. She saw him come out of the doors with a colleague. They stood at the bottom of the stairs for a few minutes finishing their conversation, and then Dan came quickly over to her.

He jumped in the passenger seat. "Hey, babe." He leaned over and gave her a kiss on the cheek. "How was your day? Any news?"

His question brought all of the sorrow from before back to Lanie's mind. Today was the day she took the pregnancy test. The two of them had been trying to have children for nearly three years now, and month after month nothing had happened.

It was hard on both of them. Lanie felt like a failure. Her siblings could all have children without any problems. Sierra, now married, already had two.

Lanie felt like one of the greatest duties of being a woman was to be a mother, and she was being robbed of that right. She also saw how excited Dan got when they talked about children. He was always so good around their nieces and nephews. He would be such a loving father, but Lanie couldn't provide that for him.

Again the guilt washed over her as she had to tell him, just as she did every month, "Not this time." She started the drive home, and her tears of disappointment started to fall.

Dan leaned over and affectionately wiped a tear off her cheek and then caressed her shoulder. "Lanie, it's all right. We'll try again. It will work out when the time is right."

Lanie was thankful for Dan's understanding, but for some reason his kindness made it even harder. She wanted to give him joy—as much joy as he had given her—but she couldn't.

When they arrived at home, Dan offered to cook. Lanie knew he was trying to cheer her up, and she was grateful she didn't have to think about what to cook for the evening. She went back to her room and lay on the bed.

As she did she knew she needed to get herself together. It wasn't fair to Dan to face this alone. They were in this together. She reached for the phone and dialed James's number.

"Hey, Lanie." James's voice washed over her as he answered. She couldn't formulate her thoughts into words. There was so much to say and none of it was coming out. "Lanie? Are you there?"

"Mmm-hmm," Lanie murmured into the phone as the tears started again.

James's voice immediately filled with concern, "Lanie, are you okay? What's wrong?"

Lanie took a deep shuddering breath and wiped her messy eyes. "I'm all right. Just sad."

James listened quietly for a few minutes and then said, "Why're you sad, Lanie?"

"I'm sad that I'm failing at my job to give Dan children." There. Lanie had said it out loud for the first time to someone.

"What? Lanie, that isn't your fault. Has Dan ever made you feel like it was?"

"No. Never."

"Right, so why are you pinning this on him? If he's never blamed you or been angry with you, you need to stop feeling guilty and depressed. From what I see, Dan treats you better than most husbands treat their wives. Don't drive a wedge that isn't there."

Lanie listened. She knew James was right. It was hard to hear; part of her wanted to just be sorry for herself, but James was a good enough friend to wake her up to her own selfishness. "I've never thought about it like that."

"Lanie," James said, his voice soft again. "I love you. So does Molly. But the person that means the most to you is Dan. You need to sort this out together. You can't keep shutting him out." Lanie was surprised again to see how well James knew her, even if they hadn't lived in the same house since high school. "Lanie?"

"Yeah?" she asked weakly. He had given her quite a bit to think about.

"Have you and Dan ever thought about adopting?" The question hung heavy in the air. Dan had brought it up a few times, but Lanie had always thought that she would be able to have her own children. It seemed like adopting would be admitting defeat. Showing the world she was broken.

"Yeah, we've mentioned it, but we've never gotten serious about it."

James must have interpreted her comment as "I've never gotten serious about it" because his answer exposed the ugly truth that she had hidden. "Lane." His voice was stern and loving all at once, something only James could manage. "Children are out there who need a loving mother and father—a home to learn and grow. Just because you didn't give birth to them doesn't mean they aren't your children."

So many emotions passed through Lanie as James was talking. She could feel deep inside that he was right. "Thanks, James. Thanks for talking with me."

"Any time, Lane. I love you."

She hung up the phone and lay on the bed for a while sorting through her own thoughts. Lanie knew that Dan wanted to adopt. He wanted to have children. Bless his heart, he never pushed her too hard, nor did he make her feel like it was her fault they were childless.

It always made Lanie's heart seize when she heard stories of people having "unplanned" children or abusing the children they had. Why were so many people given children they didn't want or deserve when people like her and Dan couldn't have the children they yearned for?

For years Lanie had ignored the pleas to adopt because she wanted to have her own children growing inside her. She wanted to feel like a mother, and it scared her when one of her friends, who had adopted several years ago, said that for the first several months she felt like she was tending someone else's child. Lanie didn't want that. She didn't think it was fair to her or to the baby.

After talking with James she had to admit that those feelings might be irrational. Yes, adopting would come with challenges, but as Dan had said many times when she voiced her fears, they could work through them—even giving birth to her own biological children would have its trials.

It was time to stop letting these fears govern her life and denying her motherhood. She may not be able to carry it, but if a baby came to her home, she would love it as her own.

Lanie stood up to go help Dan in the kitchen. She saw that he was concentrating hard on a recipe book with a mixing bowl next to him full of ingredients. Her whole body tingled with gratitude and love for this man she had married. She wanted to be better for him. He had given her so much.

She walked over and wrapped her arms around his arm and leaned onto his shoulder. "Dan?"

"Yes?" He backed away from the counter and turned so he could see her face. Lanie saw the deep lines of concern on his forehead and watched as his eyes searched her face.

"I think I want to look into adoption." She watched his face closely.

"Are you sure?" he asked hesitantly.

"Yes, I'm sure. We won't stop trying, but I think it's time to start looking for other ways to have children. I want a baby." Lanie tried to reassure Dan that she was serious about this.

Dan's face lit up like a child hearing the ice cream truck coming down the road. "Really? You mean it?" He was so full of happiness that Lanie couldn't stop herself from giggling.

"Yes, I mean it!" Why had it taken her so long to decide this? She was thankful that her husband was so understanding. She knew this decision had to be one she became personally comfortable with on her own. Nobody could force her into a decision of this magnitude.

He picked her up in a bear hug and twirled her around the room. They were both laughing and dizzy by the time he stopped.

33

Lanie Smith Dorne

Lanie and Dan waited in the hospital waiting room. It felt like they had been here for hours. Lanie looked around the room. She had brought herself a book to read, but nerves didn't allow her the concentration. The room had vinyl seats and a vending machine in the corner. Lanie wondered how many germs were floating around this room. They didn't keep the waiting room up to surgery-room cleaning standards, that was for certain.

"How long do you think it will take?" Lanie looked over at Dan. His left leg was bouncing up and down in a fast rhythm.

"I'm not sure." Dan looked over at her. "They'll come tell us if anything went wrong, right?"

"Yes, Dan. I'm sure they will," Lanie said with more conviction than she felt.

The truth was she had no idea. They were waiting for their baby girl to be born. Over the last year they had gone through the mountain of paperwork and background checks necessary to become adoptive parents, and finally the day they would get their baby was here.

It put them in an awkward position at the hospital, though. Legally they couldn't be told anything until the papers were signed, so they waited like a third wheel on date night for someone to include them.

The social worker finally came out. "Hey, you two, are you read to meet your baby girl?"

Lanie's heart fluttered. She was ready, and she wasn't, all at the same time. They followed the social worker back to a room next to the nursery. Lanie sat down in a rocking chair the nurses used to hold the babies at night when they were fussy.

"Here is your baby, Mr. and Mrs. Dorne." The social worker walked over and handed Lanie a small bundle wrapped in a pink blanket. Lanie looked down, and all she saw was beauty. Her little nose, her puffy eyes, and her skin, red from delivery. An unexpected surge of love hit Lanie as she held the baby to her chest. She had no doubt—this baby was hers.

They took the baby home, and the next day, they settled on naming her Camry. For the next few weeks and months, Dan and Lanie's lives centered around the new addition to their home. Family came to help too. It was nice to have sisters and in-laws willing to answer questions, even in the middle of the night.

Lanie couldn't imagine life without Camry.

"Lanie, I've been offered a promotion," Dan said as they were bathing Camry after dinner one day. Her wiggly four-month-old body took both of them to wash, and they both knew that it was a chance to spend time together.

Lanie looked up, surprised. "Really? That's great, Dan." She was shocked to see that Dan wasn't smiling. "What? Isn't it good?"

Dan sighed and focused on washing Camry's fingers that were constantly grabbing and flexing. "Yes, I wasn't expecting it, so when they told me I was happy."

"What did they promote you to?"

"Well, that's what's worrying me. They promoted me to office director."

"The boss?" Lanie couldn't keep the incredulous sound out of her voice. Not that she didn't believe in Dan—it was just unexpected. "What happened to the director?" Lanie worried that he had become ill or something. That would explain why Dan was hesitant about it.

"She's fine. I was promoted to be the office director of the new office in Flagstaff, Arizona." He looked up apologetically.

"Arizona? You mean all the way across the country?" Lanie was trying to make sense of it all. "What did you say?"

"Well, I told them that I would have to talk with you. Taking a job across the country is a big decision, and I wasn't about to make it without discussing it with you."

"It is a big decision. What're you thinking?" Lanie didn't want to say too much until she knew which way Dan was leaning.

"I've never thought about moving. We have such a comfortable life here. But this is a huge career opportunity for me. Not to mention the salary increase."

Lanie could tell that he had thought this through. "Dan, if you think we need to move for your career, we can work it out. I'll miss having my family close by, but Camry and I will go with you wherever you go." Lanie truly meant it, but moving away from her family would be hard. The only time she had lived more than an hour away was when she was at college.

"I know you will. I just want to do the best for our family. Tomorrow they will have more details for me, and then you and I can discuss if we want to make the move or not."

Lanie went back to washing Camry. Arizona. Never in her life did she think that she would move to Arizona.

34

Lanie Smith Dorne

It turned out that the package they offered Dan was beyond either of their imaginations. It was hard to think that they would be over fifteen hundred miles from her nearest family member, but they decided to take the job.

James and Molly offered to help drive them out. That made the stressful trip more entertaining. Lanie was also happy that they came to see where they moved; having at least one family member that could picture their life so far away made it easier.

Dan had come out a few weeks earlier and found a house for them to purchase. It was a newer build, and at the end of the street was a small lake with a walking track and a park.

"It will be perfect for Camry and other kids as they grow," he had commented excitedly as he watched her survey the new area.

He was right. It was a perfect suburban neighborhood,

just like the one Molly and James lived in. The only difference was that there were fewer trees.

Lanie did what she could to make Flagstaff feel like home, but life felt so empty to her. Dan had given her money to buy whatever furniture she needed to decorate, and that had distracted her for several weeks, but now that the house was to her liking, she realized that she had nobody—not one person—that she could invite over to see it.

Dan loved his job, and Lanie tried to hide the fact that she was not enjoying Arizona as much as he was. Her life consisted of her and Camry. She ached to have adult conversations sometimes.

She would still have her daily conversations with James, and even Molly called a few times a week, but Lanie knew they had their own busy lives to worry about. She never stayed on the phone with them for too long.

When Dan would come home from work and tell stories about his colleagues and the progress he had made, Lanie had to suppress the itch of jealousy. She had given up her comfort to come here with him. She wanted so badly to be happy, and it made her guilty to think that even after being here for almost a year she missed her family so much. The bitterness was like a slow cancer taking over her thoughts and life. She knew it was there, and knew she needed to stop it, but sometimes it was all she had that felt like her own.

She didn't want to become bitter.

She loved Dan and all that he had done for her and Camry. The life he provided for them was nearly flawless. So why wasn't she happy? What was wrong with her?

"Camry? Are you ready to eat?" She held up a jar of baby carrots for Camry to see. Camry cooed in delight and stood up unsteadily. She had become stronger and more confident in her walking skills lately. Lanie watched as her darling daughter came over, chattering something indiscernible.

Lanie put Camry in the high chair and started to feed her the carrots. For some reason Camry gagged, and before Lanie had a chance to react, Camry threw up carrots and whatever else was in her stomach all over the dining room and Lanie. Camry started to scream, most likely more scared than anything else. Lanie looked at the orange spray everywhere and started to cry herself.

Lanie picked Camry up and comforted her. She still felt a little bit warm from the fever she was running yesterday. Lanie held her, sticky carrots and all, until she felt Camry's body relax and her breathing fall into a calm sleeping rhythm.

She wiped down Camry's body and put her in her crib to sleep. She walked downstairs to start cleaning up there too. On impulse she called James at his office.

His secretary, Betty, answered, "Oh, hello, Lanie. How's that little one of yours?" Lanie had never actually met Betty, but she was always kind to her on the phone. Lanie answered a few polite questions and then waited as Betty patched her through to James's office. Betty had assured Lanie that he "wasn't busy at all."

Lanie heard James's voice on the other side. "Hey, Lane. How're you doing?" So Betty had told him Lanie was calling. Lanie was glad that she was able to sound upbeat during her conversation with the perceptive secretary.

"I'm all right. Camry just threw up carrots all over the rug in the living room." Even as she said it, it sounded humorous, although twenty minutes ago it was anything *but* funny.

"Sounds like a smelly situation. How's Dan?" James was always good to ask about Dan. Yet at the moment, Lanie selfishly didn't want to talk about him. She wanted to have James focus on her. Even as she thought that, Lanie couldn't believe how awful she would sound if she said that aloud.

She settled on something safer. "Dan is really liking the work here."

"Good. I'm glad he's liking it. How's the weather?"

Lanie knew that James was either playing along with her game of avoidance, knowing she would break soon enough, or he was distracted with work. "It's actually been really nice."

"Have you taken Camry out for a walk on the lake path yet?" Again, Lanie was thankful that Molly and James had seen their place. It made Arizona not seem like living in a foreign country where nobody could visualize where you lived, ate, and shopped.

"Not yet. Camry has not been feeling well at all. I don't dare take her out."

"That's too bad. What do you think is bothering her? Allergies?"

"No, I'm not sure. Maybe she is just getting used to the real food. Dan says she's fine, but how would he know? He's not home long enough to see her sick." Lanie felt the disdain even as she said it.

"What do you mean?"

That question opened the door for Lanie to unload the burden that she had been carrying the last several months. "I mean, I'm home all day with Camry, and all I ask is that he's home on time for dinner, and the last few days he has come home late every night."

"Why does he say he is late?"

"Work. He has some big project or something." Lanie knew that it sounded so lame and petulant as she said it.

"Lane," James said gently, "he probably does have a project."

As always, she knew James was right. It was ridiculous to imagine that Dan was doing anything other than what he said he was. He had never given her any reason to think otherwise. Yet she had all day to sit and stew and couldn't avoid her mind wandering off course.

"I know. But what if this is only the start? What if he starts coming home later and later until one day he doesn't come home at all?"

"Lanie, what are you talking about? That's not going to happen, and you know it. You're just missing him. Give him a week to finish his project, and life will go back to normal. You need to take Camry out for a walk or something so you aren't home conjuring up things to worry about. Have you been able to get some sleep lately?" James was never shy about voicing his opinion. Then again, Lanie had called him.

"No. Not much lately. And I know you're right, I just miss him. I miss all of you." Her voice sounded sad.

"I know, Lane, but it's all worth it. Just think, in a few more months Camry will be sleeping through the night, and Dan will be done with whatever project he's working on, and life will be normal again." Then, for comic relief, he said, "Go get you some friends." They both started to laugh.

"Thanks, James. I knew you would help me feel better. I get kind of hysterical sometimes."

"Anytime, Lane. Stress gets to the best of us. Now, I need to go or I'll be late for the ball game."

"Oh, yes, good luck. Let me know how it goes. Tell Molly hello for me."

Lanie finished cleaning up the orange mess from earlier. She pondered her conversation with James. She really didn't want to become bitter and angry. She knew that even before James pointed it out. She needed to do something to change before she ruined her marriage.

She sat down and wrote down several goals for herself. They included finding friends to do things with and communicating better with Dan.

When Dan arrived home, Lanie was ready to start practicing. She met him at the door. "Dan, I want to apologize." She had to get it out or she would lose her resolve.

He looked at her confused and then smiled slyly. "For what? What did you do?" He looked around the room to see if there was a painted wall or something.

Lanie slapped him lightly on the chest. "Dan! I'm being serious!"

He reached up and used his hand to mockingly wipe the smile off his face, "Oh, sorry. Why do you need to apologize?" To his credit, he was keeping a pretty straight face, but Lanie could see the mirth in his eyes.

"For being bitter and having a grudge against you."

Dan's face went serious, this time for real. "What?"

"I know it sounds bad. That's why I want to apologize. I love you so much, and I don't want anything to come between us."

Dan pulled her over to the couch so they could sit down. "Lanie, what're you talking about? What's come between us?"

Tears started to come down her face as she told him about having a hard time moving to Arizona and being a mother without help. She told him about being lonely and how jealous she was when he came home with stories of his day.

As she told him, she knew how foolish and juvenile some of her feelings were, but they were still real, and she was thankful she was letting go of them. Instead of being oppressive secrets, they were a stepping-stone for them to improve their marriage.

Dan listened the whole time, and when she was finished he didn't get mad or treat her like she was crazy. He just pulled her into him. "Lanie, I'm so sorry. I had no idea. Why didn't you tell me sooner?"

35

Lanie Smith Dorne

It wasn't as easy as Lanie wanted it to be to break some of the habits she had fallen into. She had to find a way to distract herself whenever she had a discouraged thought. She even pulled out the jogger stroller and took Camry down past the lake. Camry was thrilled with the ducks that gathered around the water's edge.

When she returned home, there was a message on the house answering machine.

"Lanie and Dan!" It was Molly. "Call me when you get a chance. I'm planning a surprise party for James's birthday and wanted to let you two know. I know that you may not be able to make it on this short of a notice, but one of the things I have asked everyone is to write or say something about James and how he has impacted their lives. Anyway, give me a call when you can. Bye!"

Lanie pulled out her cell phone. The screen saver was still the same after all these years—a photo of her and Dan on their wedding day. She dialed Molly's cell.

"Hey, Lanie. How're you doing?"

"Great! I just listened to your message. I would love to write up something."

"Thanks, Lanie. Between you and me, I came up with this idea because I've noticed James is struggling the last few weeks. I'm not sure what it is . . . he just seems to be down on himself. I'm hoping this will help him see how much he means to all of us."

Lanie felt so bad as she listened. Here she was, always calling and complaining to James, but never listening to see if he too needed help. "Molly, I'll for sure send you something. When do you need it?"

"In the next few days. I will put together a book for him to give on his birthday."

"Great. I'll tell Dan too."

"Oh, I just talked with him. When I didn't get you at the house I tried both your cell phones."

"I was out at the lake with Camry. I must not have heard your call. Thank you, Molly."

Lanie spent the rest of the day thinking of ways to write her thoughts to James. She wished so badly that she was close enough to tell him in person. Especially now that she knew he too was having a hard time. Lanie had been so lost in her own selfish problems she didn't realize she was asking for help from someone who needed healing too.

Dan came home just as they were finishing making dinner. As they ate, Lanie brought up the letters to James. "Molly said she talked with you about us sending letters to James."

"Yes, it sounds like a great idea."

"I'm going to write mine tonight so I can send it off tomorrow. If you want I can send yours with it."

Dan hesitated for a minute. "No, I think I'll send mine later."

Camry squealed and threw a piece of the bread Lanie was trying to feed her. Lanie bent down to pick it up. "Molly said that she wanted to give him a book on his birthday. Don't wait too long or it won't get there in time."

Dan's smile was mischievous when Lanie looked back up from collecting the bread. "What?" she asked, looking at his lopsided grin.

"Well, I wanted it to be a surprise later, but I know that I won't be able to hold it in." He reached into his pocket, pulled out a piece of folded paper, and handed it to Lanie.

Confused, Lanie took the paper and opened it. Flight details were printed on it. Lanie looked up, even more confused now.

"After Molly called, I looked it up and was able to get tickets for us on sale. I know I should've asked you first, but I didn't want to lose the deal."

Lanie looked down again and reread the details. "You mean, we're going to the party?" Lanie couldn't keep the tears of elation from coming. She was full of happiness, both for her husband and his thoughtfulness and to be going to see her family.

"Yes, that is what I mean. You haven't seen them in almost a year, and I think it's time we went home for a visit."

36

Vicki Scheimer Muller

Something about the phone call bothered Vicki. Vicki had never been particularly close to her father growing up, but as she matured she learned that all he did was provide the life they had. It didn't make up for all the days he missed, but she had learned to respect his efforts. They may never have a lovey sugarcoated relationship, but she wanted to show her father that she loved him.

Vicki had married Sam nearly forty years ago, who was drastically different from her father when it came to the home. He spent time with their three children and was open in his love for all of them. Throughout her marriage, she realized that her father had plenty of guilt over his lost time with her and her brother, Robert.

She had tried to reach out to bridge that gap well into adulthood. She took her children to visit him when they were small, she called him every day, and she offered for him to come visit them. She tried. Her father didn't make it easy, though.

After a while, she had to beg the children to go over. She knew her father loved them, but he didn't have experience with children. He treated them like his cadets in the military. He showed love in a different way, but try explaining that to three children under ten years old.

As her own children grew older, she resorted to daily calls to him. However, today his cough sounded horrible. One of the hard things about living over five hundred miles away was that she couldn't see what her dad was experiencing. She had to evaluate the situation with only a ten-minute call.

It worried her that he couldn't even breathe as he coughed.

She mentioned her worries to Sam. "It's so hard to know what is going on when we're so far away."

Sam listened and then said, "Did you ask Robert? Maybe he'll know something."

"No, I haven't called him yet. That's a good idea."

Vicki picked up the phone and dialed her brother. His wife, Hillary, answered the phone. Vicki had always liked Hillary. Often she wished that she and Sam lived closer to Hillary and Robert. She would have liked to spend more time with her. "Hey, Vicki."

"Good evening, Hillary. How are you doing?"

"It's a beautiful day. I can't complain. How are you and Sam?"

"We're all right too. I'm just calling to talk with Robert. I'm worried about Dad."

"Oh, no. Is there something wrong?" Vicki could hear the concern in Hillary's voice.

"I'm not sure. I was hoping Robert and I could figure out if we need to address the situation."

"All right. Let me get him for you." Vicki waited while there was rustling on the phone until she heard Robert's voice.

Robert hadn't heard the coughing. They set up a plan to call the doctor in the morning to see if their dad had told the doctor he coughed so hard he couldn't breathe. "Thanks, Robert. I'll talk with you tomorrow."

Even if she had set up a plan with Robert, Vicki couldn't let her worry go. There was a nagging feeling that she couldn't purge. On impulse she called her father one more time before it was too late in the evening.

"'Ello?" she heard her father's groggy voice answer.

"Dad. It's me. I just wanted to call and tell you good night."

"We talked earlier. Are you hurt?"

"No. We're all doing fine. How're you doing?"

As if on cue, her father started to cough. She heard his hand shuffle over the receiver trying to muffle the sound, but the coughing was so intense she thought he was going to lose his lung. There was some more shuffling, then he must've removed his hand because the sound became loud and clear. Vicki had to take the phone away from her ear the ruckus was so loud.

She listened in trepidation as the coughing quit into abrupt silence. Vicki counted the seconds in her head. "Dad?" she said into the phone. Then she heard one of the most frightening sounds that she had ever heard. Her father gasped for air. He hadn't been breathing. His inhalation sounded like a drowning person coming up for a panicked breath of air.

"Dad!" Vicki screamed loudly into the phone. "Dad! Can you hear me?"

Sam came running into the room. "Vicki, what's going on?"

Vicki didn't have time to explain; she was straining to hear her father in the background. She could hear his soft wheezing in the distance. She looked up at Sam urgently. "See if you can get an ambulance to Dad's."

37

Vicki Scheimer Muller

S*leep evaded Vicki,* even though she was so tired that her eyes were burning. She leaned her head back onto the uncomfortable seat and listened to the train's steady clacking as it sped on. It was as if she was afraid to sleep—afraid that sleep would bring on some of her worst nightmares.

She thought about the last several hours. She had listened to her father on the phone while Sam, bless his heart, figured out a way to call the paramedics near Dad's house. She stayed on the line until she heard them come into the house and take him away. She finally hung up when one paramedic must have noticed the phone lying there.

"Hello?"

"Hey! Thank you for coming." Vicki's voice cracked with emotion as she spoke to the unknown angel.

"He's in good hands," the friendly voice soothed. They took her name and number and told her the hospital they were headed to.

Vicki didn't waste any time. She found tickets to make it to her father's side. The soonest flight wasn't until morning, and Vicki's instinct told her that tomorrow would be too late. Thankfully they were able to get a ticket for her on the last high-speed commuter train between the two cities.

She arrived at the hospital groggy. She felt like she was living in some kind of dream world. The tiredness made everything feel dizzy and in slow motion.

The receptionist directed her to the intensive care unit on the fourth floor. As she stepped out of the elevator, her nostrils were assaulted with the strong scents of cleaner and medicine. *That is one way to wake up.*

She walked to the closed heavy doors with way too many informational signs for her to focus on. The only sign that interested her was the one which said, "Call for entrance." Vicki picked up the phone, and after giving her name and her father's name, the large doors opened.

She followed the nurse around the large desk to her father's room. The nurse gave her a look of sympathy and then left them alone.

Vicki parted the curtains that shielded her father from the onlookers in the hallway and had to cover her mouth to stifle the gasp. Lying on the bed before her was an old man with tubes and wires spinning off him in every possible direction. He had six different monitors beeping in rhythm.

He stirred a bit. "Vicki?"

She stepped up to his side. "Yes, I'm here." She reached for his hand. It was bruised and swollen from all the IV lines. He looked so fragile. It was hard to think this was the muscular man she called her father.

"Good. I'm not sure I have much time."

"Oh, Dad, don't say that. You're here in the hospital now."

"I can feel it . . ." He started to cough, and all the

monitors reacted in kind. The room lit up in sensory overload. Two nurses came rushing in.

They fiddled with his medicines and the monitors, and after he was done coughing they went back out. Vicki watched as her father kept his eyes shut. Even breathing was labored and pained. But he reached out for her hand again. Vicki pulled her chair close and wrapped his hand in both of hers.

"Vicki," he said hoarsely. She had to lean in to hear him. "I'm so sorry I didn't spend time with you and Robert as I should've."

Vicki didn't know how to respond. She had never heard her father be so intimate. Hot tears stung her cheeks. "Every day I watch James with his children, and I wish I would've been more like that with you." He winced as a hard breath, almost a cough, started again.

They sat there without speaking for a few minutes. Vicki watched in sadness as her father struggled to stay alive. Breathing was a determined exertion; each wisp of oxygen was a delicate pearl that had to be savored.

His hand stirred again, and this time he opened his eyes. "Vicki . . ." She leaned in farther. "Tell Robert I love him too. And . . . go to the party . . . for me."

"You can tell Robert yourself, Dad. He'll be here tomorrow." Fresh tears came down Vicki's face.

Her father shook his head. "I love you, Vicki." His voice died into a whisper, and as he shut his eyes his body went slack. The last labored breath escaped as a long exhale. Vicki's vision blurred, and she struggled to understand what had just happened. The monitors in the room flared to life again, but this time with a heavy final buzzing noise. It was over. Her father was gone.

38

Vicki Scheimer Muller

N*umbly Vicki had* signed all of the necessary paperwork before leaving the hospital. She had already called and told both Sam and Robert. They would be here in the morning. She stepped out into the early morning air. The sun was just sending welcoming rays over the tops of the nearby buildings.

"Miss? Miss, are you all right?" Vicki hadn't realized a hospital attendant was standing next to her trying to get her attention.

"Oh, sorry. I was just admiring the day."

"I just wanted to know if you needed a taxi." The attendant was still watching her with concern.

Vicki looked back at the sunrise and finally said, "Yes, I'll take a taxi."

She rode in the taxi back to the home she grew up in. It was almost seven thirty when they arrived, having fought rush hour traffic all the way from the hospital.

The yard was still immaculate. She and Robert had finally talked dad into letting them hire someone to mow the lawn. His only demand was that they didn't touch the rose garden; he would do that himself.

As she paid the driver and stepped out of the car, Vicki noted that the roses were in perfect shape still. A twinge of sadness caught her off guard when she realized that nobody would be here to care for them anymore.

She set down the small backpack of clothes she had hastily packed with her so she could dig for the spare key she always carried. Sam thought it silly that she carried it everywhere considering that they didn't live near this house. This morning she was thankful that she had it. In her rush out the door, she would have never remembered it.

She put the key in the lock and pushed the door open. The room looked like it had ever since her mother died. Vicki stood for a moment. It was a bit eerie to walk into the silent house without her father there. She finally walked in and set her bags on the sofa near the door. She took a moment to study all the photos and memorabilia that were important to her parents.

She wound her way around the room until she reached the kitchen. She wondered what her father had been eating and opened the fridge to find only the basics. He always was a Spartan when it came to meals. "Essentials. That's all you need. The rest just makes you fat," he had once told her when she had asked what he wanted to eat on his birthday.

She shut the fridge, and as she did she saw a small invitation on the fridge. She took off the camp magnet that Robert made years ago to read it. "Come to a Surprise Birthday Party for James!"

It gave details about the birthday party that was happening tomorrow evening. Like hitting a cement wall, her father's dying words slammed into her head: "Tell Robert I love him, and go to the party." She thought he must have been hallucinating as he had said it, but now she knew. He wanted her to go to the party for James.

For years, Vicki had meant to call and meet her parents' neighbors, James and Molly. They were almost more a part of her father's life than she was at times. Daily she would hear about James and Molly's three children and how they had done this or done that. Sadly, she had never taken the time to meet them. Did she dare fulfill her father's dying wish and go as a complete stranger to a party? Vicki had done some bold things in her life, but she wasn't sure she could handle this request.

What was she supposed to say? "Hi, I'm Vicki. My father's dying wish was that I come to this party?" That would scare them.

Then again, it was important enough for her father to mention. She owed it to him to do it. Vicki was happy that Sam and Robert would be here later in the day; they may even be willing to come with her.

Vicki looked around. No use sitting and moping until Sam came. She might as well start to clean.

Lost in memories of her childhood, Vicki didn't register the knock the first time. The second time it came harder and undeniable. She wondered who would be coming to visit today. She looked at her watch and noticed it was almost four o'clock. She set the shoe box of photos aside and stood up from the floor of one of the bedrooms upstairs. She dusted her jeans off and headed downstairs. She had lost track of time. Tears and laughter kept her company as she sorted through years of storage.

She opened the door to neither Sam nor Robert. Instead, a thin middle-aged woman with dark hair, dressed in scrubs, stood on the porch. The woman looked as startled as Vicki felt.

"Hello? I didn't expect anybody here. I was looking for Mr. Scheimer. I didn't know he had company."

Vicki held out her hand and then saw it had dust all over it. She quickly wiped it on her hip before she held it out again. "Hello. I'm Vicki, Gerald's daughter."

Recognition set in the woman's face and she relaxed a little bit. "That's right. I'm sorry I didn't recognize you. The last time we met was at your mother's funeral."

"I'm sorry," Vicki said, drawing a blank. "I don't recall."

The woman smiled warmly. "That's all right. There was plenty for you to worry about that day. I'm Molly. I live over there." She pointed over at the house next door. "Is your dad home? We have a party this weekend that I invited him to, and I wanted to make sure he remembered."

Tears stung Vicki's eyes—both for the loss of her father and the kindness of this dear woman and her husband.

"Are you all right?" Molly asked, suddenly concerned.

Vicki wiped away a few tears and finally said, "He passed away early this morning."

This time it was Molly who was speechless. "Oh, I'm so sorry. I had no idea." Tears were coming down her cheeks too.

"It's all right. It was just sudden. I barely made it in time. He's with Mother now." Molly nodded as Vicki spoke. "But if you don't mind I would like to come to the party."

Molly cleared her throat. "Of course. Of course you can come."

"My husband and brother should be arriving any time. I actually thought that you were them. They may join me too."

"You're all welcome. And if you need *anything,* please let me know. I'm just right there." Again she nodded to her house. Molly stepped up and gave Vicki a large hug. "If we don't see you before, see you at the party, Vicki. Again, I'm so sorry."

39

James Smith

James was rushing home from work—today was the day they were going to Troy's ceremony—when Molly called him, crying. "Molly? What's wrong?"

James knew that Molly was already home. She had picked up the kids early from school, and they were at the house. Troy and Sarah were going to drop off their children, and a babysitter was watching them for the night. The four of them would head to the airport for the three-hour flight to Los Angeles for the gala. The only thing he could think of for Molly to be crying over was the children.

"Are the kids all right?" he asked.

"They're fine, but . . . Mr. Scheimer died."

"What? When?"

"This morning. I just met Vicki at his house." James knew Vicki was Mr. Scheimer's daughter. He had never met her, but after living next to someone for ten years you learn about their family.

"That explains why he wasn't at the door yesterday morning."

"What?" Molly wasn't following him.

"He's always waiting for me at the door of the house, but yesterday morning and this morning he wasn't there. I thought that was unusual. Now I know why. Did you tell Vicki we would help her if she needed anything?"

"Yes. She said that her husband and Robert were coming in today."

"That's good."

"James, are you almost home? Troy and Sarah will be here any minute."

James pressed harder on the accelerator. "Yes, I'm already speeding. See you in a minute."

James was still dreading this whole affair tonight. He hadn't told Molly about it when Troy had told him earlier in the week. He used the excuse of the game that night, but inside he really knew it was because he still didn't want to go. It wasn't that he didn't love Troy or wasn't happy for him. It was the fact that all of Troy's successes seemed to fall into his lap. They had ever since James had known him. James had always felt like the bronze statue people winced at standing next to the shimmering gold statue they adored.

He pulled into the driveway, and Molly was in a frenzy to have him in his tuxedo as quickly as possible. Molly herself looked stunning. She was wearing a simple floor-length black gown with pearl accessories. He got distracted by the sight of her and forgot that he was supposed to be getting dressed. "Molly, you look amazing."

Molly shyly refused his compliment. "Stop it! We don't have much time." But James could see her smiling anyway. He was thankful that if he had to go to this gala, at least Molly was going with him. She seemed to brighten everything.

Sure enough, within a few minutes he heard the doorbell

ring and the riot of children as Troy and Sarah showed up. "James!" Molly called down the hall. "Troy said the company car will pick us up in three minutes."

"Almost ready!" James called back. He turned back to the mirror to get his bow tie fixed. "Three minutes? That was precise," he quipped to himself. He rushed down the hall and saw that Molly was following Troy and Sarah out the door.

"We're riding in *that*?" he heard Molly's voice carry back through the open door.

"Good-bye, kids!" James yelled into the chaotic room. Nobody acknowledged he said anything except the sitter, who apologetically shrugged her shoulders as he passed. He walked out the door and saw a sleek limousine waiting at the end of the drive. "Wonderful," James groaned.

The entire trip they were treated like royalty. At the airport, they didn't even have to pass security because the limo was allowed right onto the concourse. They drove up to the plane, and in eight small steps they were seated in luxury leather seats and airborne.

"Troy? Did you say you worked for the mafia?" James teased. With the display of extravagance, he couldn't help but be impressed and enjoy himself a bit.

Troy let out a hearty laugh. "I'm beginning to think so myself." Their conversation became just like the old days. James found himself enjoying the evening just as much as his companions. He especially liked seeing Molly so carefree and vibrant.

It had been a long time since he had seen that side of her. *We need to enjoy life more*, he thought, watching Molly animatedly recount a story from one of the children in the last few days.

As the flight continued, James found himself tuning out of the conversation and thinking, again, about his birthday.

There would be no luxury planes or black limousines waiting for him. He wondered what life would be like with all of this. What had he done wrong? Which signs in the road of life had he missed?

James wanted to give his children everything they needed to become successful people. Was he doing that? He hoped so.

Molly tapped him on the arm, ". . . right, James?" His three companions were all looking at him with expectant faces. James realized he had *totally* checked out and had no idea what they were talking about. He didn't want to admit he was daydreaming because one of them was bound to ask what he was thinking about. He couldn't come up with an alternative story fast enough, so he winged it.

"It's true if the lady says it's true," James said, rechanneling some of the cheer he was feeling earlier back into his voice.

It must have been the right thing to say because all three of them erupted in laughter. "See!" Molly said and launched right back into her story.

They arrived in Los Angeles, and another limo was waiting for them on the tarmac. They sped expertly down the streets of LA until they arrived at the venue—one of the many luxury hotels of the city. James was happy to note that Troy was just as wide-eyed at this experience as the rest of them were. *At least it hasn't gone to his head*, James thought.

They pulled up in front of the hotel, and as they stepped out, tourists stared and took photos like they were celebrities. A man dressed in a dove-tailed tuxedo approached them. "Mr. and Mrs. Walker?"

"That's us, but you can just call us Troy and Sarah."

The hotel employee grinned knowingly and nodded his head. He turned to Molly and James. "You must be Mr. and Mrs. Smith."

"Yes," Molly answered sweetly.

"Follow me." The man waved for them to follow with a wide arc of his right arm. He turned swiftly and headed through the elegant main doors. He didn't stop until they were seated at the front table of the expansive ballroom. Hundreds of tables were filling up with people.

Troy leaned over and spoke in James's ear, just above the classical music reverberating through the hall, "This is a bit showy for my tastes."

James laughed. "Well, you'd best not try and be promoted."

As the evening continued, Troy was greeted by people from all over the country. Sarah began her own line of jest. "Well, Mr. Walker, you never told me that I was married to a celebrity."

Troy laughed. "You know better than anyone that is not true."

"This really is amazing, Troy. Your company must think highly of you," Molly added genuinely.

The food was delicious, as they all had expected, and finally the program started. Mr. Eckhert stood up and made a speech about all of the people in the company and how they couldn't do it without any of them. He then paused. "Now, for the highlight of the evening, I want to invite my longest business partner up here with me. Please welcome the magnanimous Ethyl Eckhert." The crowd cheered as a woman wearing a peach gown elegantly made her way to the stage.

Once Ethyl had joined her husband, he stepped up to the microphone again. "In our company, we view you all as family. Even though the company has become larger than we ever dreamed it would become, we have some values that are important to us. These values are part of our lives and our children's lives. Every year we wanted to honor someone in the company who exemplifies those values of hard work, decency, leadership, honesty, and respect. And since Ethyl and I made this decision together, I will let my more eloquent half do the honor of presenting this year's awardee."

Mr. Eckhert stepped back and let his wife take the podium. She blinked rapidly in the bright lights. "Good evening."

James thought her voice sounded calm and reassuring. If it wasn't for all the glamour in the ballroom he could have mistaken her for someone's grandmother. "Years ago, I went out on a limb marrying a young guy with a bit of an ego." The room filled with laughter. "The only thing bigger than his ego was his dreams. Never did I expect that those dreams would bring all of you into our lives and that we would be here. Yet year after year this group seems to grow."

She shuffled nervously. "I'm not used to being up in front of so many people at once, but this is a special occasion in which Ronald and I get to honor one of our fantastic Eckhert Technology family members.

"This year we have a special person to honor. He is the youngest Eckhert employee to receive this honor. Since joining our team, he has worked hard to earn one promotion after another. His congenial personality draws people to him—employees and clients alike. He knows all of his staff by name and wishes them a happy birthday with a personal card each year. He has a lovely wife, Sarah, and they have two children. Please join me in recognizing one of our own, Troy Walker."

The room exploded into applause, and James found himself standing with the rest of them as Troy walked up onto the stage. He couldn't help be proud in that moment. He wondered why he had let his own self-esteem issues almost keep him from coming.

The room quieted down, and Troy sent a smile out to all

of them. “Thank you, Mr. and Mrs. Eckhert. I am unsure of why I deserve this honor, but I thank you. I think I speak on behalf of all here that we appreciate your kindness and hard work. And Mrs. Eckhert, it seems that you have been colluding with my wife and my office manager.” The room rolled with laughter again.

Troy continued when it had settled down. “Seriously, this is an unexpected experience. I, like all of you, come to work every day and strive to do my best. But I wouldn’t be here all on my own. My wife, Sarah, has been a support and a rock to me for years. She constantly believes in me.”

He paused and smiled widely at Sarah, who was still seated at the table with James and Molly. “However, today, Sarah and I would like to honor someone else who impacted my life long before I met her. Actually, without him, Sarah may have never dated me, and I for sure wouldn’t be here today.” James tried to think who he was talking about.

“You see, during my college days I had no direction. I lived for the next big thrill. And one day, there was a person in my life who cared enough to stop me from going the wrong direction. He was my roommate at the time, and one day he uttered words that have stayed with me ever since. He looked at me and said, after some other colorful things . . .” The room laughed again. James noted they were drinking up every word Troy sent to them. “He said, ‘You’re better than this.’ Those four words hit home for me.

“Never before had someone told me that what I was doing wasn’t enough—who told me that I could be better and do more. This person changed my life and has been an inspiration to me since. So I’d like you all to kindly greet my guest of honor and best friend, James Smith.”

James nearly had a heart attack. What was Troy doing? All James wanted to do was crawl under the table. The applause in the room was bursting his eardrums, and he was sure his face must have turned seven shades of red.

Molly kicked him under the table. "Stand up," she hissed, smiling big for the crowd and cameras that were now staring in their direction. James did as he was directed and stood up. He waved, and the applause rose again. As soon as he could, James sat back down. He could tell by the smiles on Sarah's and Molly's faces they knew this was going to happen. When Troy came back, James said, "You could've told me you were going to do that!"

Troy laughed. "Why? So you could wear a different color of tie?" He smiled broadly and clapped James on the back. "James, I know you better than that. If I would've told you I was going to do it, you wouldn't have ever stepped into that first limousine."

The rest of the evening James sat nervously in his seat. He felt like two hundred people's eyes were watching his every move. Talk about peer pressure. He was so thankful to see the black limo drive up to take them back to the airport.

As they settled in for the flight back, James looked at Troy and Sarah. "Thank you both for the wonderful night. And, Troy, you embarrassed the daylights out of me, but I appreciated your words."

"I meant every one of them, James."

James leaned his chair back and watched as the lights of Los Angeles gave way to the darkness of the Mojave Desert. It was a good night. He had never known that he had made such a difference in Troy's life. He remembered yelling at Troy that day—in fact, he'd felt guilty about it several times—but he didn't know it had been a turning point for Troy. Now, if James could just skip over his birthday, he would be just fine.

40

James Smith

The big day.

And by big day James meant the *BIG* day. Today James turned forty. He was now "over the hill," "halfway there," and "past his prime." In James's opinion, all of those euphemisms were dreary, even in jest. James didn't know what today would bring, but he was sure it wasn't something he could look forward to.

Despite his concerns over his birthday, he said many times to Molly, "Birthdays after a certain age are just another day." James had taken special care to not make a big deal of his birthday. Troy and Sarah had come back with them, and tonight they were planning on having just a small dinner—harmless.

At work, as far as he knew, nobody knew about it being his birthday. Betty would be the one to remember. He was hoping that maybe she had forgotten this year. After work he had baseball practice. His day looked like it would breeze by without any incident to bring on the mire of guilt he had been wallowing in.

James finished with his tie and went downstairs to see the children. As he hit the bottom step, he heard Natalee exclaim, "He's coming!"

Jaden chided her quickly, "Natalee! Be quiet! We can't surprise him with you being so loud." James smiled to himself. He loved his children. He walked into the kitchen, and his entire family was standing there already dressed and ready to leave for the day.

"Surprise!" they yelled in chorus. Little Noah even started laughing and waving his plastic spoon with excitement.

"Happy birthday, Dad!" Jaden said again, once the rest of the family had quieted down.

"Thank you!" James feigned surprise. "You guys spoil me."

Noah, still laughing, chanted again, "Su-pise! Su-pise!" James walked over to him on the high chair and gave him a kiss on the forehead.

"Thank you, little man. You did surprise me."

James looked up at Molly, who was standing with the children. She was smiling and said, "Happy birthday, James. Come eat before your pancakes get cold. The children have worked hard to make your breakfast."

"Yeah, and I helped Mommy make your pancakes with Mickey Mouse ears!" Natalee proudly proclaimed.

"It's true," Molly confirmed with merriment. "I was told that was the *special* way to have pancakes, and today is your special day. Jaden helped too—he cooked the bacon."

"Wow! We should have you guys cook every day." James came around and pulled Natalee and Jaden into a big bear hug. Both kids started laughing. They sat down to eat together, and James thought that at least the day was starting out on a high note.

"Daddy, we need to count your candles!" Natalee piped up cheerfully. James groaned inwardly upon hearing Natalee refer to their family tradition of counting the birthday cake candles out loud together before they all sang happy birthday. This year they would have to count forty candles for him. James was twenty numbers more than his youngest child could count.

Luckily, Molly saved James from answering. "Natalee, we'll count candles later. Daddy needs to get to work." Thankful for the save, James kissed Molly and herded the children out the door.

As they went out to the car, James started over to the newspaper on the sidewalk out of habit. He then remembered that Mr. Scheimer wasn't there anymore. Jaden noticed him going. "Are you getting the paper for Mr. Scheimer's daughter?"

"Yes, I guess so." James called back. He might as well get it for Vicki too. James could tell that his family would miss Mr. Scheimer, no matter how grouchy he was. He was a constant in their lives.

James parked the car and walked briskly up the sidewalk to work. His Mickey Mouse breakfast had put him a few minutes behind. He saw Hal and the new trainee, Kole, standing as waiting sentinels. "Good morning, Mr. James!" Hal's baritone voice carried down the street toward James. He waved and smiled back.

"Welcome to work!" Kole said brightly as he opened the door.

James laughed. "Thank you, Kole." Turning to Hal, he added, "You must be a miracle worker if you can get a young trainee to be that chipper this early in the morning." Both men laughed as he headed into the door. Now the big test—to see if Betty had remembered. If he could finish the workday without her bringing up his birthday, he would know he had been given a gift.

He walked back to his office and greeted everyone just as he did on all the other mornings. He looked up and saw Betty already passing out orders to other staff in the office. She never rested.

James felt himself hold his breath in anticipation as he walked closer, and his heart rate picked up. He felt like a small child sneaking into class late and not wanting the teacher to catch him.

Betty looked up and watched him knowingly under the reading glasses that hung off the end of her nose, though she continued to address instructions to the people standing near her. He didn't want her to mention his birthday in front of all the staff—it would spark an avalanche of questions and impromptu celebrations, and that was not something James was ready to deal with.

James gave her a smile, trying to look normal, but he just felt awkward. He passed her desk and dashed into his office as fast as he could without actually running. Once the door was closed, he let out an audible sigh. He sat down and logged into his computer. Just as the computer refreshed, his email chimed. Out of habit, he clicked open the mailbox and saw a message from Betty: "You're late." James laughed to himself again. Today was going to be a normal day after all.

James immersed himself in his work and, as he expected, the day went by rather quickly. Before he knew it, the phone on his desk buzzed. James looked up and saw the red light next to Betty's name was blinking.

"Yes?" he asked as he continued to work on the spreadsheet before him.

"Are you planning on being late to *everything* today?" James could hear the sarcasm in her voice. He laughed at her comment, to which she said, "Seriously! What do you do when I go on holiday? Your practice starts in twenty minutes. You'd better hope there isn't traffic out of the city."

James looked up at the clock, and she was right, the day had gone by faster than he thought. Practice was starting soon. He jumped up. "Thanks, Betty! And I don't know what I would do without you. That's why we pay you the big bucks!"

"Yeah, yeah . . . get out the door." He could hear her approval as she hung up the phone.

Being on the field with twelve young boys was something James had grown to like. He would describe it as both energizing and draining. The boys had an endless amount of energy, and James had to spend more time coming up with drills to keep them all active while they learned.

James looked at his phone as they were cleaning up the gear. There was a text from Molly. *Hey, Selma called and asked if Ian and Lucas could come here for a few hours after practice. I told her that you would just bring them home from the field.*

James quickly typed back, *Sure. I'm glad I checked my phone before I left.*

He turned to the boys, now almost finished, "Ian. Lucas. Your mom said that you're coming over to our house for a few hours so you'll ride home with us.

Lucas almost dropped the bat in his hand as he shouted, "Yes! That's awesome!"

James smiled. "I'm glad you're happy, but we won't be going anywhere if all of you don't get that gear put away."

As they drove home, James listened quietly to the three boys talking about the things that mattered to them the most: food, sports, friends, and the mean teachers at school. James wondered how long it would be until their focus shifted and girls rose in the ranks of importance.

As they neared the house James thought that his dreaded

birthday had gone rather smoothly. He had made it this far, and nothing was out of the ordinary from any other day—nothing to remind him of how average his life had been or how much he hadn't achieved.

41

James Smith

A*s James stopped* the car in the driveway, all three boys jumped out and ran into the house with a whoosh. James relished the silent respite for a few moments and then followed them. How they had that much energy after running around the baseball field for an hour was beyond him.

He opened the front door and immediately noticed that something was off. It was completely silent. The clamor of a growing family that usually greeted him was missing. Perplexed, he looked in and saw nothing amiss, aside from the fact that all the lights were on.

He had just seen the boys run into the house, but there was no sign of them, either. A moment of terror pushed James into action. What if something was wrong?

"Molly?" he called, setting his work stuff in a pile just inside the threshold. There was no answer. The adrenaline hummed in his ears as he hurried past the stairs and into the kitchen and living room area.

"SURPRISE!" a chorus of voices boomed at James. He skidded to a stop and tried to absorb all he was seeing, the adrenaline intensifying the shock. A sea of smiling faces looked back at him expectantly under a banner that read, "Happy 40th, James!"

James's heart sank. He was wrong. He thought he had escaped facing his birthday, yet here he was, staring at a huge crowd of people that tore his expectations of ending the day quietly to shreds. He looked quickly over their faces, searching for Molly. When he found her he saw that she too was trying to read his reaction. He knew immediately she was behind this, and, at least for her sake, he forced a smile and said, "Wow, I thought something was wrong."

It must have been the right thing to say because the room erupted into laughter and a hum of conversation. James wanted to drown into that hum. In a moment Molly was at his side. "Happy birthday, honey." She gave him a kiss.

"Thanks," he said, still in a daze. "When did you have time to pull this off?" He looked around and saw Paul, Olivia, and Sierra and their families, his parents, and then he saw Betty. She must have known about this the entire time. No wonder she was willing to not say anything about his birthday at work. She didn't want to ruin the surprise.

Molly smiled with glee. "I've been planning for a few weeks. I was hoping nobody would slip up and tell you."

James pointed out Betty greeting Hal and a woman James assumed was Hal's wife. "How did you get people from work here?" Now that he was able to focus on faces instead of an overwhelming group, he saw a few other colleagues in the crowd.

Molly laughed and wrapped her arm though his to walk him out onto the patio in the backyard. "Betty," she answered. She didn't need to add anymore; they both knew that one word was enough to accomplish any task. When they stepped out into the yard, James's panic returned. There were even more people outside. Molly must have invited everyone James knew.

He saw Selma chatting with Jessica and Jessica's husband. "You're sneaky."

Molly looked up in mock surprise, "Who, me?'

"Yes. I can see how innocent you act after asking me to bring Selma's boys home. I never thought to ask why . . . I'll know better next time." He couldn't help but smile as he teased. Molly looked genuinely proud of her accomplishment. As much as he was revolting against this party, he didn't want to ruin it for Molly. He could survive one evening. Hopefully.

Just then James saw Lanie and Dan walking up the steps toward them. "What the . . .?" He didn't finish his sentence before he was off to sweep a giggling Lanie up in a hug.

"When? How did you get here?" He was shocked to see his little sister. They didn't have many secrets they could keep from each other. Even when they were little, they would tell each other what Christmas gifts they were going to exchange because they couldn't handle the suspense of keeping a secret. "Didn't I just talk with you a few days ago?"

Lanie and Molly laughed. Lanie stepped out of the hug to rejoin Dan and said, "Yes! You did talk to me. I didn't know either. I guess we married two people full of surprises." Lanie hit a grinning Dan playfully on the chest and reached down to hold his hand.

"It's so good to see you. It's just unexpected." James cut himself short of saying that he would rather have Dan and Lanie here and not all these other people so the four of them could catch up on life, but he was still mindful of Molly's work. He turned to Molly. "You've really been busy."

Before Molly could answer, Sarah and Troy walked up and joined them, "Hey, old boy! Happy birthday!"

"You too?" James said with an exaggerated eye roll at Molly.

Troy belted out one of his hearty trademark laughs. "Yes, us too!"

"How long have you known about this?"

Molly quickly answered, "Well, when Sarah called to tell me about the gala in Los Angeles I told her about this idea and—"

Sarah cut in, "And we decided that we could join the two events and then spend a few days with family here in the city and be here for your party."

The pieces started to come together for James, and he wondered how he had missed it. "So that's why you insisted on being picked up here in the city instead of us coming to you?" This time he addressed Troy.

Troy gave a strong sidearm hug on James and said, "You've got it now! But we need to get started. Is it about time, Molly? I'm assuming these people didn't come just to eat the food."

Molly nodded, and Troy steered James off to the other side of the patio that overlooked the yard. James put some pressure on Troy's arm to stop. "Wait, what're we doing?"

Troy only smiled, and then before James could object again, he bellowed, "Hey, everybody!" He waited for a second, then yelled again, "Everybody! We want to get started if you want to join us out on the lawn." Little by little the conversations died down and people filed passed Troy and James out to the lawn. Many of them said some small gesture of congratulations to James as they passed. He couldn't help but think that this was his funeral, and all these people had come to watch.

All this time James itched to ask Troy what they were

doing, but he knew it was a fruitless line of questioning. He was gathering by where they stood that there was some kind of pending program. James liked this idea less and less the more people gathered. They were all people he knew, but that didn't make him like it any better.

Once most of the people were down on the lawn, Troy said, "Thank you all for coming. As you know it is James's birthday, and Molly invited us all here to celebrate the man that we all love." James wanted to turn around and walk back into the house. He had hundreds of eyes boring into his soul. He felt self-conscious and exposed, like he was naked on a platform.

Troy continued, "Now, we all know James—some of us for years, others for a few months. But one thing we all have in common is that James has made an impact in our lives." Troy turned to James but talked loudly enough for the audience. "Molly asked us all to write a letter to you about what you mean to us. I know that sounds cheesy, but we have each enjoyed reflecting on the way you have improved our lives."

James could feel the red of embarrassment creeping its way up his neck and filling his cheeks. To say he was uncomfortable was an understatement—he was mortified. He almost wished it *was* his funeral. Troy looked past James and nodded. James turned to see what Troy was looking at. Jaden and Ian walked up with two large binders. They handed one to Troy and one to James.

Troy held it up for those to see on the lawn. "James, these two binders are a collection of our letters. These are some of the expressions of gratitude that we have for you being in our lives." James opened the binder in his hands, thankful to have a reason to look down. He flipped through a few pages and saw letters to him from all the people standing a few feet from him.

"Molly has also asked if some of us wanted to say something to the crowd. I told people at the gala how much you mean to me and Sarah, but for the group here I will repeat again some of my thoughts about James.

"James changed my life. He and I met on our first day of college as undergraduate freshman. For two years I partied, chased girls, and did everything that my parents trained me not to do and nothing that had to do with school. I was tumbling out of control to a disastrous end, and I had no plans to stop. It was James, who usually did his thing and stayed out of my business, who exposed my denial to the problems I was creating for myself.

"James is a true friend. He could have easily let me go and moved in with someone else at the next chance. But he didn't. He wasn't the type of friend I'm afraid that I was to everyone else—he truly cared about me. His genuine concern for me awoke the realization that I was not becoming the man my mother and father had sacrificed for me to become." Troy paused for a few seconds and cleared his throat from the emotions.

He started again with a deep passionate voice. "Without James I wouldn't be where I am." He paused again to catch his breath and smiled. "But enough about me. Who wants to go first?"

Betty, who was nearest to the patio stepped up. "I'll start. Someone has to." She started up the three stairs to join them.

Troy greeted her cheerfully, "Thank you! If you, and all of you that come up, will share your name and how you know James so we all know, that would be great." Much to James's gratitude, Troy then led him down to join the crowd on the lawn. If he was going to be "roasted," he would rather be down here where people couldn't study his reactions.

"Very well," Betty started. "I'm Betty Lioneti, and I have kept James in line at work for as long as he has worked there." She looked over at Molly. "And, Molly, I can tell you I feel bad for the work you must do here at home for him." The crowd exploded in laughter at Betty's wit.

"Seriously, though, I've enjoyed working with James. He's a wonderful boss. I've been with Near World for more years than I can count, and James is the best. I knew it from the day he started as a young skinny boy." Again, a wave of chuckles rippled through the crowd. "I've liked working with him so much that I decided to stay in my position. I've been offered retirement and different 'promotions,'" Betty said, putting up her fingers in air quotes, "several times, and I've turned them all down. I figure I like my work, I like my boss, I'm old, so why move now?

"I've watched James lead his team. He is ethical and fair, and most of all he knows us all by name. None of us mind doing as he asks, because he treats us with respect." Betty turned to face James. "So James, I know I'm hard on you sometimes, but I want you to know I appreciate you as a boss and as a friend. I feel privileged to tell others that I work for you. Thank you, James."

She smiled and added, "Now, if you get promoted, and I'm sure you will—either that or I've bet on the wrong race horse—I expect you to take me with you."

With that she stepped down the stairs to join everyone again, and they offered her a soft applause with their laughter. Betty walked over to James and gave him a big hug.

James watched as Betty faded into the group. Her words surprised him. He and Betty had a good working relationship, but he didn't realize that Betty had not retired or taken a promotion just to stay in his office. It both flattered James and made him understand that he could invest more time in learning about his employees and their lives outside of work. He made a mental note to start.

James was brought out of his thought when a deep voice

nervously said, "Well, I guess I'll follow Betty since I work with Mr. James too." James looked up and saw that Hal and his wife had replaced Betty and were now addressing the crowd. Hal's wife—Frances, if James remembered right—was beautiful for her age. She had one arm around Hal's arm and shuffled her feet with tension. Obviously neither of them was accustomed to being in front of a large group.

Hal continued, "But I . . . we . . . felt it was important to share our story. James has really made a difference in our lives." James was again caught off guard by Hal's comment, and he saw that Frances, a person he only knew through a few brief conversations with her husband, nodded emphatically in agreement. James tried to think of a way that he'd helped these two. Unlike with Betty, where his frequent interaction lent itself to an expected comment, Hal threw him off. He waited to hear what Hal would say.

"You see, I've worked for nearly twenty-nine years at Near World with some of you." He pulled Frances closer. "And this is my wife, Frances. We have five children, and we are happy to say that all, except for our baby in high school, are either in college or finished. That's one of the reasons we are here tonight." Now James was really confused. "I've worked for years at a job that is most often thankless. I see people come and go all day. I've learned their names and tried to bring some happiness.

"I don't do this to get praise, I do it because it also brings me happiness. However, most of those people could see me out on the street out of my Near World uniform, and they wouldn't know me from the next man. But Mr. James is different. Every morning Mr. James looks at me directly and calls me by name and asks how my day has been. Nobody else does that. Even as a doorman, I can see that Mr. James cares about me; he doesn't just treat me like a part of the building facade."

James suddenly became thankful that years ago his parents had stressed that you treat everyone with respect and love—no matter their rank or wealth. He hadn't even thought twice about learning Hal's name. It just made sense. How can you not learn about a person you see at least three times a day? James wondered how many times he *did* pass someone and didn't say anything.

Hal became quiet for a moment. "But that's not why I came up here today. I came here to say that James saved my job. As we mentioned earlier, we have five children. When we were married, we set a goal that our children would get a chance to attend college. That was something Frances and I weren't able to do. Life has been hard. We have worked hard every day of our lives to create a better life for our children.

"Our first two children, Jackson and Rhonda, are now finished with college." James could hear the distinct love and pride in Hal's voice that only a father can have. "Our next two are in college now, and our youngest is a high school senior. Our dream to have educated children was becoming a reality. However, when Near World announced cutbacks, we were devastated. When Mr. Barnes said that layoffs were pending, I was literally sick. I knew that when it comes to essential staff, a doorman isn't high on the list."

Hal stopped and started to choke up. Frances wiped a tear from her eyes too and pulled Hal closer as if supporting him. James watched the tender scene in front of him. He could feel his already fragile emotions stirring.

Finally, Hal cleared his throat and began again with a raspy passionate voice, "What father wants to go home and tell his family that he's losing his job? Who wants to think that after twenty-nine years of serving as one of the most exposed invisible employees of a company, he is going to be *let go?* There are no words to describe the feelings of failure that come with the prospect of everything you worked for just vanishing with your dreams attached."

Hal's voice was thick with ache now. It was raw truth. James looked at the crowd near him and saw that the entire group was fixed on the beautiful crying couple on the patio. All of them were completely quiet. Some of them were also wiping tears from their eyes. Listening to Hal, James thought about the way he had been feeling over the last few weeks and realized life wasn't as bad as it could be. The reality is that he only had a 10 percent pay cut, but people like Hal nearly lost their entire livelihood.

Hal continued, "The feelings of failure and depression were indescribable those few days as we waited for the inevitable news that I was being laid off. It got so we even hated checking the mail. We had to tell our three youngest children that they might have to drop out of school."

Hal paused again with a deep inhalation. "The day we received the news that Mr. James had created a plan to save our jobs, I was so full of thanks. We still didn't know if the board would pass it or not, but I was full of hope. Not hope for my job—I didn't dare hope for that until I heard official word—but it was a hope for mankind. It meant the world to know that someone was fighting for us. Someone cared enough about us to keep looking for ways to not lay off families.

"Mr. James showed me that even though he works on the top floor and I on the sidewalk, I still mattered." Frances started to stir beside Hal. Hal looked over and nodded. "Go ahead, Mamma."

Frances stepped forward a bit and wrung her hands nervously. "Mr. James," she said in a timid singsong voice, "Hal and I have prayed every night since that day for you and your family. We know the sacrifice that you, and all the other board members, must be making so we can provide for our family—people you've never met. We, Hal and I, wanted to thank you for thinking of us. Thank you for helping us achieve our dreams." She stepped back to Hal, and they held each other as they descended the stairs. In contrast to Betty's exit, the crowd was now quietly sniffing.

Someone hugged James's arm. He saw that at some point Molly had joined him at his side. She had tears in her eyes and squeezed his arm with loving approval again. Hearing Hal's story, James, for the first time, had peace with the decision to take a pay cut.

There was a commotion across the crowd from where James and Molly were standing. James saw that people were moving aside to allow someone through the crowd. He watched until, at last, Selma Tobin walked up to the patio.

Selma paused and wiped her already tearful eyes. She smiled weakly. "I should've gone before you, Hal. I didn't want to cry when I did this, and here I am crying already." They all laughed politely as Selma's humor gave them a change in emotional pace. "I, like those earlier, have come here to share my appreciation for Molly and James—James especially."

James thought that this night was getting more and more interesting. These weren't the people he would've expected to stand up.

He was getting to know Selma's boys better as the baseball season progressed, but he didn't know Selma herself. Watching Selma being up there was even more baffling than it was with Hal and Frances. He had no clue where this would go.

"My name is Selma Tobin. I have known Molly and James for a few years as our sons, Ian and Jaden, have been friends at school. This year my two boys have been playing on James's baseball team. You may know that I'm a single mom of two active boys, ages eight and ten. I have tried to give my boys the most normal life possible, yet I still couldn't provide everything that they needed." Selma paused and James could see she was a bit uncomfortable with sharing something so intimate with complete strangers. His heart filled with compassion for her.

"My boys are growing and will someday be men. I realized that with all my efforts, I was still only a single mom. Without a father to show them how to become upstanding men, I was afraid they would fall into looking up to unrespectable men. I didn't want that. I want them to learn what it means to lead, to be kind, to love, and to work. Several nights I lay awake trying to figure out a way to handle the situation.

"One day, the answer came in an unexpected way and in a very stressful time in my life. Molly called and asked if Ian and Lucas would like to join their son, Jaden, on James's baseball team. There were so many reasons that I knew this wasn't a good idea—I was worried about time and money, both of which always seem depleted and stretched thin in my life. But then I thought back to all the times I had seen James interact with both Molly and their children. These were only brief experiences, yet it was still enough to know the type of man James was. There have been a limitless number of men in my life that are bad examples, and James had none of those qualities. He was the type of man I envisioned my boys becoming like someday."

As Selma paused to gather her thoughts, she folded and unfolded her arms several times. "The decision to have my boys play on James's baseball team was one of the hardest but best decisions of my life. The sacrifice of time and money was an investment into my boys' future. Since the beginning of the baseball season, James and his family have become a frequent topic of discussion. My boys are not only learning about work ethic and teamwork to achieve goals through playing a sport, they are seeing what good men are like.

"For example, at the game this week, I knew that it must have been tempting to take out Lucas, the smallest child on the team, in order to win. But you didn't. I wanted so badly for my son to succeed, and it hurt to watch him cross the field in sorrow after we had lost the game. James," Selma said, giving James an apologetic look, "even after all the good you have done for us, I still misjudged you that day. I saw you walking swiftly to Lucas from the dugout, and I assumed, based on my past with men, that you were going to chastise and berate him for his performance. I ran, protectively, as fast as I could from my seat to defend Lucas when you arrived. To my surprise, you didn't yell. You didn't scold. I was stunned as you dropped to your knees and hugged my child and cried with him. Not many coaches, or men for that matter, would do what you did that day.

"As a mother, I want to thank James for selflessly giving his time. Even if you didn't know it, you are shaping my sons and making our home a better place. They have been given a different perspective on family life." Selma started to tear up again. "Thank you, Molly and James, for letting us be part of your lives. As a single mother, I appreciate all the help I can get." Selma gave both of them a quick nod and then stepped off the patio in a rush.

James was touched by Selma's words. He thought back to practices and games. He never, that he knew, treated Ian and Lucas any different than the other players. The only experience that stuck out was giving Lucas a hug at the game a few days ago. At the time, that hug was more for him than anyone. He was glad, once again, that he had done the right thing without even knowing it.

Lanie stood up next. She bounced up the patio stairs with Camry on her hip. Much like Betty, she seemed perfectly comfortable on the patio speaking. She wiped her eyes quickly and laughed softly. "With all this crying, I feel like this is a funeral." The crowd laughed with her. James smiled. He could always count on Lanie to understand how he would feel. "I'm Lanie, James's sister." She looked at Camry, who was curiously looking at all the new faces on the lawn. "And this is my daughter, Camry. We recently moved to Arizona when my husband, Dan, was transferred there for work.

"I don't want to take up too much time up here, but I did want to tell James how much he means to me." She stopped and took a deep breath, and James saw a few tears come down her face. "I wasn't going to cry," Lanie said, half laughing. She wiped her eyes with the back of her hand. "James and I have been friends as long as I can remember. We are so close in age, I guess it was inevitable. As kids we used to get into trouble together and, of course, blame it on each other when Mom would ask who did it." The crowd snickered with her.

Lanie looked over and smiled at James. James smiled back. She was right; they did get into quite a bit of trouble when they were younger. It was a miracle they didn't send their mother to her grave early due to stress.

"But those stories will be for another time. Today I want to tell James thank you for being such a support to me throughout my life. Next to Dan, James is my biggest cheerleader. When I am having a hard time or just need to talk with someone, I always know James is there." Lanie held Camry up a little bit higher. "In fact, Camry wouldn't be part of our lives if it wasn't for James and his willingness to tell me to shape up and stop moping around. Through James, I learned I need to face life and enjoy it. I have to stand up and actively seek a solution. No problem solves itself. It takes dedication, flexibility, and faith."

Lanie looked over at him and Molly again and added, "Molly, I want you to know that I'm so happy James married you. I think all of us, as his siblings, would tell you that you are a perfect match for him. You two are a perfect couple. Thanks for being part of the family. Once again, happy birthday, James! I'm glad that Molly and Dan contrived a way for us to be here." She stepped down off the stage and the group shifted a bit and hummed with their conversations.

A few seconds went by and James saw them stirring. Nobody walked up to the patio, which James was grateful for. The words that had been said were beautiful and heartfelt, but James was anxious with all of the attention. He was glad Molly was standing next to him. Lanie was right—Molly was a perfect match for him. She got him to do things he would never do on his own. This party was only one example.

James exhaled with relief when he saw Troy stand up on the patio. Troy began to thank everyone for sharing their thoughts when a voice from the crowd interrupted him.

"Excuse me. May I say something?" James turned, with everyone else, to see who had spoken.

"Sure you can. Come right up here," Troy invited. James saw a woman he had never met walk shyly up beside Troy. Troy stood for a few seconds and then stepped away, signifying the opportunity was hers. They all watched as the woman tried to figure out how to start. She opened her mouth a few times, but closed it again after nothing came out. She choked back some tears and covered her mouth with her hand until she was calm again.

Finally she said, "I don't know any of you. I only met Molly a few days ago." James looked quizzically at Molly, who only nodded in agreement and turned back to watch the woman. "My name is Vicki Muller, and I grew up in the house next door." She pointed to Mr. Scheimer's home, and James understood who she was—Mr. Scheimer's daughter. Molly had said they had met. "My brother and I now live in different cities, but my parents lived here next to Molly and James for years. My mother died a few years ago and my father . . ." She stopped and pulled a tissue out of her pocket to dab a new wave of tears. "My father passed away two days ago."

An audible sympathetic gasp came from the group. James wondered why Vicki was up there; it must be torture for her to do this. "I was lucky enough to make it here only a few minutes before he died. The reason I decided to talk today was not to depress you, but because I wanted James and Molly to know how much their family meant to my parents and to Robert and I."

James felt like he was playing that groundhog game at the arcade—just when you think you can't be surprised again, another one pops up and is more shocking than its predecessors. What Vicki was saying made no sense at all. James replayed all of the morning "conversations" with Mr. Scheimer in his head. They were never pleasant or even friendly. James was actually sure that Mr. Scheimer detested them as parents.

Vicki continued by addressing them directly. "James and Molly, I'm sorry that I didn't come and meet you before this. I hope that we can get to know each other better. Every day I called my father on the phone, and he always had a story about you and your family. I feel like I know you through those conversations.

"Dad was in the military for years, and he never quite let the gruff military mentality go. Even with my own children, he showed love in the tough-love kind of way, so I'm sure that you felt some of that too."

Molly moved beside him and James knew that she too was thinking of all the times that Mr. Scheimer had growled at the children or told them how they were parenting wrong. "It took me a few years into adulthood to learn that he had a unique way of showing love. That's the main reason I wanted to get up and talk today.

"James, I want you and Molly to know how much your family helped my dad. After Mom died, he was really lonely. Sadly, he was also too prideful to admit it or move in with Robert or me. We have our own families away from here, so it was your family that kept him company.

"For example," Vicki said, turning from Molly and James to address the crowd again, "Dad planned his whole day around being up for the moment James brought the paper to his door."

James was floored. He had no idea that Mr. Scheimer had cared. "Dad also liked to tell me stories of watching the children play in the yard. When we were growing up, he was often gone with work, so he missed those days watching us play in the yard or running in the sprinklers. I think he felt guilty over that, and by watching your children do it, he could re-live the moments he missed.

"Dad was always telling me how good of parents you two were. He would constantly drop hints about you, James, and how he wished that he would've been more of a father like you are."

Again, James was stunned. Mr. Scheimer was always telling James how to parent better. James started to wonder if he had been total strangers with this neighbor.

"I want to say thank you on behalf of our family to both of you for making him feel included, even if it was as awkward as I imagine it must've been sometimes." She let a coy scoff escape. "He was so proud of any invitation you extended for him to join in on parties and events. Even today's party." Fresh tears again. "Today, he wanted to be here so badly. He had the invitation Molly gave him on his refrigerator, and one of the last things he told me was to make sure I attended tonight. That is how much he loved your family. Right after telling me that he loved me and Robert, he asked that I come tonight and share his love.

"It is hard for me to be up here, but I would be doing him a disservice to not fulfill his dying wishes. So, thank you both for including my father and helping him feel loved when we were too far away to do it ourselves."

James watched Vicki walk back and join two men standing in the crowd. Molly had said that her husband and brother were coming. Throughout all those days of picking up a newspaper and smiling through Mr. Scheimer's slights, he never expected the man was actually appreciative.

Troy jumped back up on the stage. "Thank you, Vicki. Our prayers will be with you and your family during this time. Now, I just want to bring one last person up here to the stage. I think it only appropriate we end the party with her. Molly, will you join me?"

Troy opened his hand to invite her up. James felt Molly tense. This wasn't planned, obviously. He smiled to himself—at least Troy was going to put her on the spot as she had put him on the spot all night. Troy waved again. "Come on, Molly. You planned this whole event to honor James, and who better to end the night than you?"

Molly grudgingly joined Troy at the patio. "You sneak." She hit him on the arm.

Troy laughed and quipped right back, "I do believe that James called you the very same thing earlier today." The group laughed again.

Molly turned to face them all. "I suppose Troy is right. I should say something. Before that, I want to thank you all for coming. Tonight has turned out to be better than I had imagined. So thank you." Molly turned directly to James. "James, I love you and hope you realize how much you mean to all of us here. Even after all our ups and downs over the last thirteen years, I'm still thankful I married you.

"I've watched you work hard to provide for our family. I've seen you spend time with our children or help me around the house after you have had a long day at work, and I have seen the genuine man you are inside and out. The people who shared today have proved that you make a difference."

James's thoughts went to the wording on the bathroom mirror that had caused him such anxiety over the past several months. Molly must have put it there as a gesture of kindness. He had read it completely wrong.

"On your birthday, James, we all want to let you know that we appreciate all the simple and kind deeds you do each day. Those kind deeds, that seem so small to you, make a world of difference to us. Happy birthday, honey. I love you!"

42
James Smith

T*oday was James's* first day of being forty years old. Surprisingly he felt younger and more energized today than he had in months. Last night had been a paradigm shift for him. He realized that he had missed the value that his life had. Often he had strained to see the good in one aspect of his life and myopically missed the very object he had looked for. He had assumed his "ordinary" life hadn't accomplished everything that it "should have" accomplished.

Thanks to Molly's surprise party and Troy's gala, James learned that even ordinary acts can have an extraordinary impact on others, and he may never know it. James knew he had been offered a valuable gift, and the effect was twofold.

First, he knew he could stop moping about and start to live each day to the fullest. For the longest time, he felt that he was in a rush to go nowhere. He now realized something that he had known all along—no person is worthless. Through daily interactions, everyone assists one another through adversity.

Second, James made a personal goal to start looking outside his own worries and insecurities and find others to serve. All the letters, and especially those that spoke last night, showed James how the small acts he never really thought about changed their lives. He set a goal to actively seek to help, instead of just passively helping. He wanted to learn more about his employees, become closer to his neighbors, and most of all develop stronger relationships with his family.

As James got out of bed, he suddenly found himself welcoming the idea of being forty. If the past day was any indication, life would be anything but ordinary.

Discussion Questions

1. Which character in *Counting Candles* do you identify with the most? Why?

2. Each character in *Counting Candles* has moments when they reach out to help someone else. Is there ever a time when you have given help or a time when you received help?

3. Do you agree with Shamanda's decision to not tell her family about her problems? Why?

4. What are some of the underlying themes throughout *Counting Candles*?

5. What are some experiences in your life that may seem ordinary but were actually extraordinary?

6. The characters in *Counting Candles* all struggle with self-worth in one way or another, but each of them came to realize they did matter and were important to someone. Which character did you feel learned that the most?

7. Some of the characters conceal their deepest personal issues, for example Lanie not telling her husband she was

depressed or James admitting he felt useless and mediocre. How would their lives be different if they had asked for help?

8. Why do you think Gerald felt so close to James and Molly's family but kept them at a distance?

9. *Counting Candles* portrays several marriages. Which couple's relationship impacted you the most? Why?

10. James Smith's view of his life and actions were not the same as others' perception; he was his own self-critic. Why do you think that is?

11. Several of the characters in *Counting Candles* felt inadequate, weak, or hopeless. These feelings curtailed their true success. Why do those feelings have such an impact? How is that habit broken?

12. In *Counting Candles*, answers to prayers and problems come through others. How can you be an answer to someone's prayers?

13. Most often we neglect to show love and appreciation to those closest to us. Why is that?

14. The quote Molly chose to put up on the mirror was "You make a difference." Why do you think she chose that quote?

About the Author

Being raised in a small farming community, Dustin W. Bradshaw thrives on adventure and challenge. Dustin lives by the theme, "If you want to accomplish something, do it!" It was with this attitude that Dustin penned his first book in third grade and, as a senior in high school, entered and won a literary scholarship that he was told no male has ever won. This same adventurous nature has helped Dustin achieve many of his life's goals, including forming that country boy into an accomplished leader. Dustin is now a foreign service officer for the United States Department of State. He and his wife, Lady Hiva, are now posted in Manila, Philippines, and will soon be posted to Istanbul, Turkey.

You can find more about Dustin or *Counting Candles* at the author's website www.dustinbradshaw.com or on his blog, www.dtbradshaw.blogspot.com.

0 26575 14337 9